CHATEAU MARMONT

WAITING
FOR
LIPCHITZ
AT

CHATEAU
MARMONT

A
NOVEL
BY
**ARIS
JANIGIAN**

A Vireo Book
an imprint of Rare Bird Books
Manufactured in the United States of America

Distributed by Publishers Group West
a division of the Perseus Books Group

Design by Jacques Alimonte

Publisher's Cataloging-in-Publication data
Names: Janigian, Aris.
Title: Waiting for Lipchitz at Chateau Marmont : a novel /
by Aris Janigian.
Identifiers: ISBN 978-1-942600-19-0
Description: A Vireo Book | First Hardcover Edition | Los Angeles
[California] ; New York [New York] : Rare Bird Books, 2016.
Subjects: LCSH: Chateau Marmont (Hollywood, Calif.)—Fiction. | Hollywood (Los Angeles, Calif.)—Fiction. | Fresno (Calif.)—Fiction. | Screenwriters—Fiction. | Architecture—Fiction. | BISAC: FICTION/Literary.
Classification: LCC: PS3610.A569 .W35 2016 | DCC: 813.6—dc23.

I'd just about given up and l
a metropolis. I'd even gone s
220 miles away in Fresno, t
nowhere texted, "Nxt 2sdy,

etermined to leave for good this bestial excuse for

as to put down a security deposit for an apartment

-called armpit of California, when Lipchitz out of

ont, 12:15?" Immediately I was sucked into the light of the lantern, a magic lantern that had seduced, addled, and nearly incinerated me, just as it had seduced, addled, and incinerated millions of people before me and would continue to do the same to tens of millions more well into the future. This realization, that I was merely one among countless dreamers, the worst sort of hypnotized American moth tumbled in from out of nowhere, and not a serious screenwriter born and bred in Los Angeles, alas, made me feel at once sick to my stomach and part of a community, even a kind of ravaged diaspora now spinning in small cynical circles everywhere in the world. I had arrived an hour early because I wanted some time alone to gather my thoughts, and to put some of them aside, especially those having to do with my great friend (and so-called LA novelist) John Hirschman, who had moved to Fresno a year before, as if to light a path for me there.

But maybe it wasn't such a good idea to arrive early, I now thought, because it was possible that Lipchitz was staying at the hotel—industry standard for Angelenos who want to decompress or conduct business or other sordid affairs away from the prying eyes of family or associates—and would spot me sitting at the bar on his way out or in from one or another of the Chateau's little hideaways. My early arrival would signal a damaged state, which reflected my state precisely and the reason it concerned me at all; an early arriving writer clearly had time on their hands and a writer with time on their hands was by simple logic low in demand; ample reason for Lipchitz to take ruthless advantage of me instinctively and indeed justifiably as a shark takes advantage of sea life bleeding. I could just see him spotting me waiting at the Chateau and veering aside to put in a quick call to one or another of my fellow writers to gather intel: "What's the four-one-one on…these days," and one of my cohorts saying that as far as they knew I was no longer with CAA and that they'd heard, not sure if it was true, I was fairly

ARIS JANIGIAN

depressed and had even given thought of moving away, and that, maybe they were wrong, I hadn't landed anything in over five years. In any case, I'd already determined my bottom line for the script, which, by even current industry standards was debasingly low, and since I no longer had an agent I would be able to hang on to another ten percent, so the amount I received wasn't so much in question as was control of the product. What I most wanted, I suppose, was money for the rewrite, because income, any income at this point, would allow me to postpone or shelve altogether my move to Fresno that I had already wholeheartedly, or so I thought, embraced. Prima facie, the move would seal my fate as a screenwriter, because any move to a California county outside of, perhaps, Santa Barbara, was a virtual sign of retirement, and a move to Fresno was tantamount to checking into a convalescent facility, the career equivalent of one of those horrifying stucco structures with rattling window fans and foul-smelling hallways and cottage-cheese ceiling dining rooms where Jamaican nursing assistants three times a day convey in the human refuse for their turkey sandwiches and grapefruit in a plastic cup. I would have to quickly cancel my thirty-day notice, a potential problem as my manager, a once-upon-a-time successful commercial actor doing mostly sports ads—tennis rackets and golf balls and running shoes—nearly peed from glee when I told him I was moving out of his basement room, what I called, even to his face, The Dungeon. For years he'd earned a tidy living from residuals, but then the gray set in and our interminable sun's toll showed on his still ridiculously handsome face and now all that bottled up ego went into answering complaints, collecting rent, vetting potential tenants, and occasionally booting them out. Bottom line: there was nothing that he relished more than a groveling renter, especially a once-upon-a-time successful screenwriter, and he was near jizzing to have me out of there so that he could clear the way for another beautiful—if not *superbeautiful*—actress, and, yes, it should be one word, as *superbeautiful* is the status of these ontological women, the very essence of their being…and also, I think it's fair to add, in most cases, their very eventual nothingness. Wouldn't it be sweet to not rescind but rather leisurely convey to the once-upon-a-time that I would still be leaving, not to Fresno (as I had absentmindedly mentioned), but rather to a house I purchased in, say, Los Feliz, as my most recent script was just picked up for a sum, obscenely large goes without saying.

The beautiful waitress (were there any other kind here? Honestly, even homely women in LA managed a kind of nebulous beauty) finally came by and took my order: vodka martini with a lemon twist. Why not? How I would relish depositing such glorious news at the once-upon-a-time's doorstep, and how I would relish more or less saying/doing the same to half a dozen other acquaintances, and—*frankly*—friends, who, one by one as my career took on ventilator status, no longer came by or even called in fear of picking up the dreadful virus that was ravaging them as well but not so immaculately and swiftly as it was ravaging me, because, let me be clear: while most of them were just victims of a sea change fiasco affecting the entire industry, my victimization was also self-inflicted. After selling three movies three years in a row (my last, *The Reddest Storm*, about the nineteenth century Belgian King Leopold and his genocide of the Congolese—an Academy nominee for Best Original Dramatic Screenplay), I had reached, by any industry standard, A-list status: clubs and dinners and flying here and there to festivals, major or minor made no difference, and lodging and quaffing five-star and finally returning to a gorgeous modernist house-on-stilts in the Hills with any number of equally gorgeous and streamlined women. It was an impressive run of fun, and finally I took my accountant's advice and put a little money away in real estate—a two story Tudor in Hancock Park—instead of throwing gobs of it forever into decadence and rent. This would be 2007, and my ruin. Six years later I was wondering whether my vertically blue striped cotton shirt (Macy's Spring Men's, circa— *also*—2007) would date me and my decline… and, thrilled that I had found a parking space, what a luxury, on Sunset in front of the Chateau, bypassing the ungodly parking fee of thirty dollars a day, which turned into a day after merely three hours, what I believed at the time was going to be about right for my visit with Lipchitz. I now reviewed my plans for refreshing my meter: ten minutes before the one hour countdown, citing irritable bowel, for Jewish screenwriters a credible malady, I would excuse myself and race down to Sunset and stick another eight quarters into the mocking mouth of the machine—mocking because I no longer even had a credit card to swipe into in its new and improved credit card taking format—and make my way back up pausing in the Chateau's gorgeous bathroom to rinse any sweat from my face. I worried that Lipchitz would detect that I could no longer muster the schoolboy enthusiasm that is a prerequisite for striking a Hollywood deal, because the moment one slips into pessimism, much less cynicism, the moment one can no longer muster the gusto of the bubbliest world class bullshitter is the precise moment the entire apparatus moves away from you in loathing, as there is nothing more alarming to the industry, more shattering to the core, than someone who cannot muster the necessary enthusiastic unctuousness to keep the whirligig spinning, just the right zesty insight or clever guffaw or wisecrack to emolliate the egos of the magic lantern wunderkinds.

Across from me now sat a super skinny guy, late twenties, with a straggly beard and sunglasses and Fred Segal-ish white linen shirt. Beneath his yellow slacks, with a high-end cotton satiny sheen, he wore yellow socks and aqua blue burlap fabric shoes. Crossing one skinny leg sharply over the other, he continued on his cell phone rather loudly, as if to convey that so accustomed was he to owning whatever space he found himself in that he considered even the bar at the Marmont his. I listened, not particularly because I wanted to, to his discussion with his associate about how X was very interested, and how X had looked at the script and wasn't joking around, and how he'd been waiting for a part like this and felt that it was very much what his career needed at this point, but the deal was X wanted a part of the action, and that *that* was the big question here, whether part of the action was on the table, and that *that* was what the person on the other line needed to think about, really consider seriously, because he had the feeling that X was being serious, no bullshit was involved here, and that they needed to get back to X pronto, because word was he was considering another project, not really the kind of thing he wanted right now in his career, especially after the butt fucking—let's be *honest*—he took with Z, but still he was considering it, and that you know how things go, one day he'd be considering it and the next day he'd be locking the other deal in, so really seriously think about what slice of the pie we might give X on the back end. The hot air of the conversation was going of its own internal combustion, apparently, because he kept turning the issue over and over, as though its sheer recitation was intoxicating, like he was sticking his dick into a new orifice of the same old guttered Hollywood whore each and every time he said it, this way and that. Listening in on all this hyping and jockeying much less irritated and impressed me than it depressed me, because

I realized above and beyond everything else that, again, I no longer had the enthusiasm to orgy thus and that Lipchitz was bound to gauge it as accurately as a Geiger counter measures radiation in a room.

When I came up from this thought, the angular young man was recoiling from whatever it was his associate was now ramming into his ear, his boyish face all full of boyish worry, and when he finally spoke again the voice had turned boyish, too: "Okay, man, sorry...I just, you know, want to lock this deal in..." and "Yeah, yeah, yeah, hey, take your time, we're good, no worries; cool, we'll talk when we talk." There it is: he's been pissed on. The fear that he'd pushed too hard was writ large all over his pretty straggly bearded face. The one hit, or—more likely—one bunt wonder, was taking a deal that was a complete hypothetical, if not an out-and-out fantasy, way more seriously than he'd earned the right to. Suddenly he stood, all concerned and cornered, and the skinny little nobody that he was all along in his Fred Segal-ish outfit came into wretched relief. I nodded politely when our eyes met, but he was in no shape to respond, as he fumbled for his iPad that he'd left on the side table and tramped away through tepid puddles of his associate's piss. Don't worry, Skinny Jeans, you're hardly alone: Hollywood's cold merciless money hand has everyone shaking in its boots. Money is no longer a thing in the hands of someone; it's a thing that has everyone in its hand. It doesn't flow through the economy; we flow through *it*. It isn't sitting on a table next to a character in a movie; it's the character in the movie with the human, if not the whole of humanity, waiting piously in the pews for instruction. Make the wrong move and risk banishment to where whole generations of writers, like myself, have effectively been banished to a kind of movie-making gulag. Even though we journeymen, so to speak, were willing to compromise and do whatever was required, it wasn't enough, because fresher and more tender flesh like you were prancing through the door with their dicks in hand, happy to do whatever the doctor ordered with it—even if it meant sticking it in Hollywood's shattering hole. I pictured the countless number of skinny novitiates in tight-fitting yellow jeans turning to crisp, even as I sipped my martini, in mid-air, just as I had turned to near crisp in mid-air. Still, I vouch as both witness and participant, for how despairing the city renders you, every crime committed upon your mortal soul is ready to heal and the deepest gratitude approaching amazing grace floods over you for something even as small as a call back. A good ninety-five percent of the city survives solely on the ridiculously infinitesimal and remote; in fact, the ridiculously infinitesimal and remote is very nearly the only oxygen Hollywood breathes. Even the now-and-then extra, virtual Hollywood quarks and crumbs are on the verge of one or another life-altering deal that is so incongruous with the observable world that its mystery belongs to the realm of quantum mechanics. So many deals are about to happen, if but one in ten thousand actually did, the industry would collapse under their collective weight; but under their collective non-weight the city takes on a kind of sick buoyancy. I now extrapolated from the dozens I knew to the desperate mass of thousands, if not tens of thousands, of actors-turned-writers so that they might act in their own movies; and when that didn't pan out they turned actor/writer/director, and when that didn't pan out they turned actor/writer/director/producer, and more than half of those probably went so far as to outlandishly add distributor to their title. If all that fails, and it almost always does, you became a novelist, because once your novel becomes a bestseller you can easily parlay that into a script, and if that proves impossible you can do a graphic novel (same parlay thinking), or even a children's book (animation voice-over potential here), and if you can't make it as any of the above, in a last ditch effort to salvage your ego you can join the ranks of memoirists and describe your long and laborious journey to oblivion, which would make a dynamite movie with a powerful narrative arc that you will naturally star in! Indeed, to accurately describe this state of verge a new word might be coined, perhaps *vergitego*—yes, the ego left on the cliff's dizzying precipice until the skin is raw and eyes are cooked to sockets and all that is left are buttons and yarn and a few strands of hay; in essence, a near human wraith that any stray wind should be able to blow away—yet, bizarrely, hardly a cyclone could budge an iota. In sum, so mixed up is the human psychology in this city that the intrusion of reality rather than modify psychosis actually amplifies it.

My father, the bookkeeper, who counted a handful of studio execs as clients, saw the madhouse for what it was. Since my days as the co-editor-in-chief, alongside Hirschman, of Fairfax High's *Colonial Gazette*, all I wanted was to be a writer, especially a screenwriter, but at my father's urging, even demanding, I decided for a supposedly safer and more rationale career choice.

After graduating from Columbia with an MA in journalism, I landed at the Cleveland *Plain Dealer* where I worked for five years. I was in the thick of reporting on a series of local government corruption scandals when I got a call from the *LA Times* asking if would I be "interested in returning home." My mother, the ever garrulous and get-around-town-girl, had quieted down to Shabbat Temple and Bob's Coffee and Donuts at the Farmer's Market on Monday morning with her girlfriends, what I dubbed the Fairfax Four; otherwise she was cemented to her apartment couch reading *The New Yorker* and the *New York Review of Books*, watching the classics on VHS, and listening to KUSC and *Bookworm*. "I don't have the appetite, anymore," she'd tell me, and about time, I'd think, because her so-called appetite that, however cultured, I can only describe as rapacious and indiscriminate, had destroyed her marriage and disaffected me for years.

"It would be nice to have you around," she admitted, when I told her I might be moving back, a stunning reveal as she showed absolutely no interest in having me close to home before; in fact, her interest was in keeping me as far away as possible so that she could do what she wanted to do, for however long, at whatever hour, and at whatever the price, while hacking through as many disgusting and ultimately lethal packs (my guess was three) of Virginia Slims she wanted to a day. Maybe, I thought, we'd finally have a chance to sit down and put it all behind us, and what a long catching up it would prove, since we hadn't, I swear, had a face-to-face since I was eight, when, all at once, tired of the dishes, the scrubbing, the cooking, the cleaning and mending, she folded up her apron and marched out of the house. "I needed that," she exhaled, when after midnight she returned, though what *that* was was a mystery and remained one as my dad offered no interrogatory, merely an imperative: "Don't get used to it."

Old Toad, Stick In The Mud, and Mr. Doom and Gloom were a few of the choice nicknames she slapped on my poor father—a decent man who probably should've left his bookkeeping practice at the office—as she zipped out the door for a lecture at the Goethe Institute, or an exhibit at MOCA, or a Zen meditation class up at the Vedanta Center, or a ten-dollar demitasse of oolong at that new tea place on Third Street, one of a seemingly endless series of outings, real or fabricated—just to get away from us—was anyone's guess. The woman's greatest fear was coming to a stop long enough to reflect in earnest what she had taken in. No, it wasn't a matter of absorbing and synthesizing moments so much as passing through them, or rather letting them pass through her like water passes through the slippery lungs of a shark.

At the *Times*, I joined the city desk, and almost immediately a story I'd written was optioned and made into a full-length feature film, returning me on the *back end*—from which I would also finally get expunged—what I made in a year in salary. If it was easy to write a story that could be turned into a screenplay, how hard could it be to write a screenplay from scratch? I had a knack for dialogue and an even greater knack for dramatic pacing, so much so that I began to wonder whether my return wasn't written in the stars, as they say. I left the *Times* just months before that real estate homunculus, a world class Shylock, took the helm. The pillaging and slaughter and mass graves that reduced that great paper into what it is today—a battered, driveling, backwater village rag—is now an old story and barely worth mentioning, but I still found myself incensed at how in such short order its big, thick, ballsy coverage of breaking events had turned into a scrawny, ridiculous, effeminate retelling of everything already quite obvious to everyone. In between these thoughts,

I was taking in the glamorous riffraff: mid-level brownnosers, rosy vegans, Bentley-driving yoginis, and leaders of one or another production cult, in loose fitting linen or super tight jeans, their air of soft exhaustion all mixed up with SS level remorselessness, the twitter and rustle and barely muted mania of their brains pushing me to the brink of fight or flight. How impossibly welcome neurosis was here, in fact, my meeting with Lipchitz, when it was all said and done, would most likely amount to nothing short of a negotiation with a neurosis, as were all industry meetings in LA, with the actual person barely squeezing into the room. Yes, everyone brings their best neurosis to the table and with all their neuroses laid out the deal-making begins in earnest.

I began to feel my bowels agitate just thinking about it, and so I kind of jogged to the bathroom with my script in hand. Sitting on the Chateaus' john for one minute, then two, with hardly a plop, I wondered what living amidst all this toney mercilessness had done to me, what the unending stuns to my insides spelled for my long-term health. It no longer had to be the case but I was making it the case, as if the past five months I'd spent deliberating and finally concluding I had to leave LA had amounted to spinning in place.

As though my dear friend John Hirschman and the world that he'd shaped in Fresno in advance of me, and even *for* me, had amounted to nothing.

The southern edge of The Great Central Valley began a little more than a hundred miles from Los Angeles, the same distance to Santa Barbara or San Diego, yet, as I drove to Hirschman's farm house that day, I was forced to admit that for decades I had dissed, dismissed, or better omitted it from my consciousness. Honestly, I had a more full spectrum image of the Mojave and its monotonous and hopeless sand than I had of the most prodigious stretch of agriculture in the world and in world history. It was, for me, a cultural and artistic desolation between the two stellar poles of LA and SF, and—like almost everyone—when I travelled north I took the wide and monochrome 5 rather than the 99 with its acre after acre of farmland, shacks, rambunctious pickups, and scandalous flare-ups of cow dung. It was a place where even radio offered no refuge: Mexican Ranchero, ZZ Top-era rock, redneck conspiracy theorists, and religious millenialists, the kind that bellowed from big tents in the revival days of old, covered it. This relentless battery of insults amounted to a "fuck you," a belligerent refutation of everything we north and south progressives, with our caucuses and causes—free trade coffee and gluten-free galettes—stood for. Even the names the Central Valley folks chose for themselves, let's be frank, next to the singsongs of Santa Barbara or Monterrey or Santa Cruz, not to mention San Francisco, were two syllable curses, self-defeating monstrosities: Wasco and Arvin, Shafter and Goshen, and, no kidding, even a place called Weed Patch—all bad, but not nearly as bad as Fresno, that sounded like something Fresh that was actually rotting at the core. How could I forget, when I was nine, or maybe it was ten, travelling through Fresno (before the 41 freeway was built) with my mother and father and aunt on our way to Yosemite where we were going to stay at the famous Tenaya Lodge. We exited the 99 somewhere downtown and started up Blackstone Boulevard, what proved an interminable stretch of small hotels and shopping malls and gas stations and fast-food stops. As the vista opened up and we climbed the rolling golden foothills heading out of town, Mom, who'd been dead silent, came roaring back to life: "I'd go out of my mind if I had to live in a place like that. What do people do in Fresno? Gas up and go from one Jack In The Box to the next?"

"I'm sure there are things to do here," Dad said.

"What?" Mom pressed on, "Drive tractors and milk cows. I feel like I need to wash myself off."

This prompted my aunt from the backseat to weirdly say, "I bet you could count the number of Jews here on one hand."

"Of course they don't live here," Mom emphatically agreed. "Jews don't farm." She might've been puffing dirt from her mouth for how repulsive it sounded.

"Why don't Jews farm?" I asked.

"We leave that to other people," she said.

"Because," my aunt clarified, "the goyem didn't let us own land."

"Has nothing to do with it," Dad demurred. "That's all a myth. Plenty of Jews work here as fruit and vegetable brokers and wholesalers."

"But they don't farm," my mom insisted.

"No, for the most part, that's true, and the reason is brokers and wholesalers are lower risk jobs, and there's better money at it. If farming made better money we'd be doing that, too."

With that recollection, I wiped, though there was nothing really to wipe, and washed and dried my hands on the Chateau's fabulous cloth towels and returned to my seat at the bar where I ordered my second martini.

Hirschman had assured me his place would be easy to find, as all the roads and avenues in the country were numbered to the halves ("If you can count, you can find it...")—but my GPS got *Road* mixed up with *Avenue*, and by the time I reached Avenue 12 and Road 29 ½, I'd lost forty-five minutes and nearly all confidence to negotiate the last leg. ("Just past the railroad tracks you'll see a fruit stand and a mailbox. Turn left there and go down a long dirt driveway running between cherry trees. My place is at the end of the drive. You can't miss it because it's the only house.")

As it turned out, nothing to fret over, I was off the road and threading the orchard and inside of a minute rolling up to his farm house that was actually a trailer home, maybe thirty years old, and forty-five feet long by fifteen or so wide. From the eaves of the super deep porch, which ran the entire length of the trailer, he'd hung the head of a rusted shovel, an axe, a lantern, a small kettle, a wash board, a spade, a sprinkler head, a bottle opener, and other odd objects—I'd learn a little later—he'd discovered abandoned or even buried around the farm. From the copper tone of his skin, he looked to have spent a good deal of time broiling under that September sun, which hovered, just then, near or in the triple digits, I guessed.

"You found it!" he said, kind of surprised, making me think. "So, it wasn't so easy as fucking counting after all!"

Deliberately leaving my frustration, but also—I should add—my duffel bag behind, I walked up the stairs and onto the porch where Hirschman greeted me with a big backslapping bear hug. Chattering a mile a minute about what a bounty he'd harvested and what a feast I was in store for, he brushed me inside where instantly I was hit with a thick briny mélange of smells that, along with the ceiling that was eight feet high at most, made me feel sealed in against my will.

"Take a seat," he said, on a mid-1990s Southwestern-style couch featuring four ugly pink Navajo diamonds evenly spaced on a washed-out field of green. It was facing off with a burly forty-inch TV threatening to smash its cabinet, a tiny particleboard one with charcoal tinted glass doors. To complete the appointments, all sourced, I thought, from the local Goodwill or the like, there was a faux leather lounger, splitting apart, and not just at the seams, and next to it a Home Depot–quality shelving unit crammed to the point of catastrophe with VHSs and DVDs. A single air conditioning wall unit just off the door, with a few colorful streamers to show it was blowing, was enough to do keep the place quite comfortably cool. The kitchen, from which the briny effluences were obviously coming, was situated at the far west end of the trailer, and he looked to be in the middle of a food chemistry project, what with the beakers and measuring cups and pots and pans and tongs and stirring spoons and mason jars. I'd never known Hirschman to cook so much as an egg, and here he was bottling, sauces and salsas and soups and stews, aside from pickling a dozen different vegetables. Basically, anything he could grab from his garden to feed him through the winter and spring, he'd crammed into maybe a hundred Mason jars, alternately the color of mud, blood, and lagoons that were cooling and curing on every surface, including the linoleum floor. Interposed between the jars on the floor were about a dozen cardboard boxes brimming with fresh vegetables he'd harvested over the past week alone, some of which maybe weren't so fresh if the gnats pulsing over them like dancing water fountains were any indication. His new *lifestyle*, as they call it, was either a symptom of an extended manic episode or the manifestation of a spiritual sea change, a kind of crossing over, he told me. And what a crossing over it would prove, as nobody I knew had spent as much time obsessing over and circumnavigating LA: its back alley eateries and bars and other dives; its remotest subcultures, from the Santa Muerta cult to, I kid you not, Tuvan throat singers; its mountain passages that even Google Maps gave up on; and especially its architecture, buildings—both living and dead, breathtaking and utter eyesores—which, if read correctly and in *toto* (impossible, obviously), told the story of Los Angeles from front to back, he always claimed. How could he leave all that hard-earned and gritty city know-how for simple grit?

Now, there, in Madera, whose name I'd rightly, as it turned out, traced back to the Portuguese *Madeira*, a slight chill ran up my spine, and I found myself reflexively looking beyond the front door for an escape hatch should it come to that. Yes, so bizarre did the atmosphere seem, for a tick I wondered whether Hirschman might soon be sizing me up for bottling, too. I'd always been intimidated by Hirschman, whom I considered a force of nature. If he were an animal on Noah's ark they would only need one of him. Spending any length of time with Hirschman, I invariably found myself thinking and even speaking like Hirschman, at which point I would vaguely panic and have to switch subjects or flat out flee to salvage whatever I could of my own thinking and speaking. But there were also times listening to Hirschman that I had the sense that I was, in fact, listening to my own thinking when whatever it was that kept me from saying it or thinking it was sent packing. In any case, it was obvious that Hirschman was not in his right mind. In fact, as long as I'd known Hirschman, he'd proven utterly out of his mind, what just then seemed the only explanation for how he'd ended up here against the counsel of his closest friends. I was concocting excuses for why I'd have to renege on my promise to visit for three days—not so easy as anything work-related was obviously off the table—when he reached into a box and pulled out a tomato and told me its weird name, Wapsipinicon Peach, and for the next hour or so the tour continued, covering way too much produce for him to possibly eat, the reason for the bottling, or for me to possibly remember, but which I've reconstructed here from copious notes I took during that visit.

For tomatoes, of the rarer varieties, he had Brandywine, Hillbilly, German Green, and Black Krim, which was the color of coagulated blood, and, honestly, when shined up on his shirt one of the loveliest fruits I'd ever seen. Squashes: all the usual suspects, but also Guatemalan Blue Banana, which was big as a small canoe, and Butternut Rogosa Violina (what a beautiful name!), and Galeux d'Eysine, and Yokahama, forest green color and sunken in at the stem like someone had pulled its plug.

He had strange cucumbers: one sickle-shaped with runnels running it's hooked length, Armenian, and one the size of a tennis ball…and almost as hairy, called so because of its color—lemon. On the corn side, there was Oaxacan Green, and Golden Bantam, and Bloody Butcher, with ruby red kernels that gave it its bloody name! He claimed a dozen melons, including Charleston Grey, and Klondike Blue Ribbon, and one with a beautiful bluish green hue, yellow freckles and a big yellow patch, that he picked up gently as a babe; its was called Moon and Stars, originally from Kentucky, he told me, thumping its belly for ripeness—*perfect!*

There were Kurdish White beets and Chioggia; he cut one in half and showed me the lovely red and white concentric circles that brought to mind a candy cane. ("I pickle them to death," he said.) And there were Japanese and Taiwanese eggplant, and the most voluptuous radiant Black Beauty eggplants that he proudly piled in his arms like he meant to make a harem of them.

On the leafy side of things, he had Red Malabar spinach (red, for its stems, he noted) and French Sorrel that he ate straight or stirred last minute into soups, and Red Russian Kale, and Osaka Mustard with black-purple leaves big enough to use for a fan in a pinch. He had a bean called Cherokee Trail of Tears because the Cherokee had taken them on their long, sad march to Oklahoma, I discovered; and Asian Red Noodle beans long as shoestrings, and a purple carrot actually called Cosmic Purple. ("Eat a couple of those a day and you'll live longer than you'd care to.")

Of the many herbs he had piled in a box, he was especially proud of his basils: Purple Petra, Genovese, and Holy Basil from India that he planted in front of the trailer home because it attracted, he claimed, good spirits. It was like I was sitting there as he introduced, one by one, all the tribes of America gathered for a powwow, or as though he were a medium conjuring spirits far and wide and lost to time, which wasn't far off the mark as he'd soured these seeds from amateur gardeners that had held onto them sometimes for generations.

"And look at these," he sort of screamed, stabbing an arm into his freezer and pulling out a foot-long frozen thing, and then another, until the RABBITS were stacked in his arm like the wood he intended to roast them with. He'd shot and shucked them right there in the orchard. I was "probably wondering the whereabouts of his books and LPs," he told me. (Given all the other data I was struggling to process, I hadn't noticed up until then that the entirety of his vast and vastly interesting collection had been reduced to a single five-tiered shelf just off of his front door.) What happened there was that when he decided to move to the farmhouse, he went back to LA and did what he wanted to do for years: slim down his collection to what mattered—maybe a hundred books that, by now, were like old friends that he'd now and again want to visit with—and took the balance to one of the last remaining bookstores. They knew who he was, of course, and so the two owners followed him to his U-Haul asking what he was next up to writing-wise, and as they sifted and sorted through the boxes, he went around the corner for a beer, finding he was a little sad parting with his long time acquaintances but knowing too it was the right thing to do. When he returned an hour later to see how it was going, about fifteen boxes were there on the ground, and a small pile, maybe thirty books, set aside.

"That's it. That's all you want to take?"

"So far," they answered.

"Out of all these boxes? Do you even know what you're looking through,?"

He start popping open lids and pulling books out: "*Monks and Love In Twelfth-Century France*...okay, maybe the audience there's limited, but look, here's Piaget's *The Moral Judgment of the Child*, a classic in developmental psychology....and how about a nice copy of *Faust*. What is it, nobody reads *Faust* anymore? Huxley's *The Perennial Philosophy* changed my life, and Rilke's *Wartime Letters*. How rare is *that!* Don't you have enough of those vampire novels or werewolf or whatever miscreation of the month it is? Do you really need another copy of *Fifty Shades*?" he asked them.

"We have to be very particular about what we buy these days; things have changed, and our markup is near nothing what with Amazon and Ebay," they kvetched.

"Well, what are you going to pay me for them?"

They swung their two heads left and right, puckered thoughtfully, and one guy, too spryly for Hirschman's taste, said, "How about two dollars a book?" Whereupon Hirschman started loading the truck back up, the two so-called book buyers, stunned that he would reject their offer especially as they'd spent over an hour culling (as in good fruit from bad). But after getting the same culling treatment from another dealer clear on the other end of town, the reality that that was about it struck him like a frying pan to the side of his head—he might've put them in storage, but storage, it turned out, was just about as expensive as the farmhouse he hoped to rent, and so he decided to donate (as though he needed a *tax write-off!*), thinking first of his local library on Sunset where he now schlepped his books only to find people were unloading books to the point they hadn't the staff to sort through what they already had. That he might attest to this heartbreak with his own eyes, the librarian took him to a storage room where boxes of books just like his were stacked floor to miserable ceiling. He knew serious books were a hard sell, but he had no idea you couldn't even give them away.

Now, he let his fingers do the walking, as they say, and finally the librarian at the Mid-Wilshire Branch said, "Sure, bring them in," and so he drove over there and went to find her, all full of a hope. She followed him out to the truck and went through about half a dozen boxes, picking through them like she was picking through a fucking dumpster and said, "Can't use these, but thanks for thinking of us!"

Again, Hirschman: "Do you have any idea what is here! What important books these are? Look at this!" He kind of stabbed *The Other Victorians* at her, at which point she started to worry he'd go ballistic on her. She suggested two other libraries, but Hirschman had already contacted them.

"Yes," she said. "It is true: nobody was accepting books at this time."

"At what time will you all be accepting books?" he asked.

"Hopefully, at some point," was her soul-altering answer. Now what was he going to do? Could it be he got the idea in a twisted way from the librarian, because in a fit of what he described as *informed rage*, he started driving around and unloading them into actual dumpsters, one box at a time, all over town, until he'd gotten rid of nearly fifty boxes, ten alone in a dumpster behind the Ralphs at Beverly and La Brea where he felt what he could only describe as a *sick exultation*, a revenge that moved in two directions at once, toward the world that had rejected these books and toward himself that was trashing them. It was then that that sick exultation made him simply sick to his stomach, and it occurred to him: *Why not take them to skid row!*

So he backtracked and retrieved all the boxes he'd dumped, drove downtown, and got a couple of homeless guys who were standing there to help him unload, he himself looking, one imagines, near homeless at this juncture for what it took to retrieve the books from the dumpsters. Slowly, people started coming at the books, one, then two, then a dozen and more. Seeing how appreciative they were, he'd never been happier, and the great thing was that not a single one of them knew who he was or what he'd written; but then after about forty-five minutes they stopped coming, the bookish type among the area homeless apparently exhausted.

The boxes were open and books were falling out, oh, probably two thousand, right there on the sidewalk, a monumental clutter—and if he were to stay there to take blame, he imagined the even more monumental littering citation, so he got in his truck and drove away. Last he'd seen of those books.

Listening to him tell this story, the commerce-minded Jew in me began making a calculation of the loss, the staggering loss in economic terms far more than in cultural terms. "You threw away a good ten thousand dollars worth of books?"

He countered, "More like two thousand at today's prices. Maybe if I held on to them for a generation they'd become collectables, like vinyl, but it wasn't adding up—what with the crazy cost of storage. I confess," he said, "it was a kind of suicide." And so it seemed was his simple moving to Madera, all of it of one piece.

It started with him just wanting to get away for a few weeks after pushing for months on end to find a readership for his newest novel on Los Angeles, and so he headed to San Francisco where several friends lived. For a week, he took in the city, its coffee and pastry shops and bookstores and bars and working wharfs, what few there were left, and all the rest…and then he headed home thinking that maybe after having lived the entirety of his forty years in LA it was time to make a move. He couldn't think of living outside of California, and outside of SF and LA there obviously wasn't another city to live where—however lovely, as in San Luis Obispo or Monterrey—he wouldn't fall sleep. That day the 5 was narrowed to one lane for repair, so he crossed over to the 99 via the 152 in Los Banos to continue his route South. Coming into Fresno, he exited Shaw Avenue for gas, and it was there at a Chevron Station that he saw a big sign across the street that read: *Open Today—Forestiere's Underground Gardens.* That it would be a thing of artistic or cultural or even visual importance never entered his imagination, still, he wondered what the hell an underground garden might be. He pictured a big cave with hundreds of potted plants hanging from rafters—and then, just as soon as he wondered it, the pump tripped full and he needed to get moving along…to Los Angeles—but, in fact, he didn't even want to go back to Los Angeles. He didn't want to be in San Francisco, and he didn't want to be in Los Angeles, so there he was in Fresno

It was early springtime and every hour—*on* the hour—tours were going, but that day he was the only one in line, and he felt kind of sad for old Forestiere the gardener, whatever it was that he'd done underground that nobody cared to pay attention to that day. He passed under a large stone archway and proceeded down a ramp and entered the main room where Forestiere had hosted many large parties and banquets, the guide told him. Baldassari was an Italian immigrant (and also, apparently, though unmarried, a sociable one) who had come to America with a capital A in mind, what he could bring to it and what he could obviously bring to himself. So, at the age of thirty, he purchased eighty acres to farm only to discover the hardpan beneath the topsoil was impenetrable, a root killer. Now what was the man to do? Remembering the catacombs and wine cellars in Italy, how they kept the barrels and bottles cool, he figured to dig a room to at least escape the mauling valley heat. It worked exceedingly well, the temperature and quality of air down there fair as fall, and now seeing what he could do, he kept at it for the next forty years, as though he'd unleashed some inner-mole.

For something built underground, the main room was impressive for its size, otherwise nothing to write home about, but as he was guided deeper into the complex, passing beneath sturdy stone arches and through softly curving corridors, his amazement grew at what this man with a simple shovel, axe, wheelbarrow—and no serious training in architecture or engineering—was able to achieve, and even more mind-boggling, over ten acres and at three different levels. He'd carved a sitting area with a lovely fireplace for him to greet his guests, and a full on kitchen with a stove and basin and arched cubbyhole where he'd tucked a green icebox. Hirschman went down a flight of stairs to find a room with an overhead aquarium, not in working order, but still…the image of the man sitting there and looking up, through a plate of glass where his tropical fish once-upon-a-time swam was amazing. Here and there the home made white plaster was chipped and failing revealing the stones, hardpan broken into workable sizes, arranged in every combination, and the mud that held it together, as well as the chisel and axe marks, like memory made manifest of the sacrifice and labor it took. From overhead, light fell through channels onto interior courtyards with stone planters holding trees and oranges and peaches and carob and jujube (a kind of date) and loquat, a few, just then blossoming, their jasmine scent drifting down a hundred corridors, some narrowed to accelerate and others widened to slow the air, or even curved and split to move the air in two or three directions at once. There was a little chapel and a courtyard with a triangle-shaped planter that signified the Holy Trinity, and from the center of that planter a massive and gnarled vine twisted and turned like the body of Jesus on the cross.

Yes, as Hirschman described it, by the time he reached the master bedroom he could very nearly feel Forestiere's presence down there, to the point that he was even imbued with gratitude, as in,

"Dear Baldassari, thank you for your labors!" It was a quite large bedroom, with a bathtub and a washstand with flowers growing next to it. Two or so feet off the floor, maybe to keep some bugs away, his mattress and blankets were tucked inside a large horizontal cavity. They planted a spotlight at the foot of the bed and the way it illuminated where his body once lay was like something out of a Caravaggio. It was a place both to lie and die. Just below and to the side of that bed he'd fashioned a simple hearth. Hirschman stood a good long time studying it, carrying on what would amount to a life-changing conversation with it, until the guide more or less booted him out. He thanked the guide profusely for her intelligent exposition, however much she were a volunteer, as well as her willingness to leave him to peruse a few of the rooms alone, and then said adieu. He left that afternoon thinking mightily about life and death, about art, the kind of art that comes of a lone man chiseling away year after year according to a homegrown vision and how different that was from the kind of art he and the vast majority of his peers had been doing: what the difference was and what did it mean?

I took in the beautiful almost lit-from-within guests in the Chateau and pictured us, Hirschman and I, having a late lunch on his patio, with the pummeling sun turning the air wavy with heat. On a rickety picnic table he set a large plate with Armenian string cheese, locally-made flat bread, a medley of cucumber, tomatoes, and peppers dressed with local red wine vinegar and olive oil. We'd just started in when he said, "I'd trekked way into the redwoods, and burnt incense in great Buddhist temples, and I'd even knelt for prayer in Catholic monasteries, but honestly, I'd never felt anything like I did in Forestiere's gardens. Or, at least never felt it with such weightiness, a weightiness that crushed me and at the same time pried me open, like a nut. After Forestiere, I, and what my craft had turned into, almost instantaneously sickened me, and I saw quite clearly how the whole writing scene—in fact, all so-called high culture—was utterly devoid of, if not a total assault on Forestiere's ethic, and amounted to a complex farce. Not that these farce makers and farce funders, these art raconteurs, would even recognize Forestiere as competition. In fact, it's an old story: When a person is forced underground and works alone to bring their vision to fruition, no sooner do they open their doors and welcome people in that those same people pretend not to notice that they're there—much less that they've fashioned (behind their backs and without their stamp of approval) a work of virtuosity. Because artists of Forestiere's caliber and sensibility, naturally and quite innocently, are too busy, and, in fact, born ill-suited to pay homage to the art raconteurs, the raconteurs pretend not to notice the man or the work, and then when the man is dead they quietly try to bury that work, demolish that work, treating it no better than common dirt. A person like Forestiere whose whole life was dedicated to letting in the light is an affront to and, even more, a repudiation of these mole-whores whose only goal is to thwart the passage of anything resembling light except as it falls on their everlastingly shivering egos. Look at what's happened to writing, serious writing, like they supposedly teach at these writing schools today. After graduating from college with earnest ambition, if not a fierce will to tell their stories and express their pent up brains, most—if not all— would-be writers enter these MFA programs, where your chief goal is to fully tool up in order to ass-lick your way into a career upon graduation. Diploma in hand, you now have the pedigree to apply alongside hundreds of other ass-lickers for publications and prizes and grants, all judged by ass-lickers who also teach in these programs, but under higher titles, naturally—Associate or Full Ass-Licker. After licking hundreds of asses, if you're lucky, you might get an Assistant ass-licking position where you can in turn get your ass licked by those coming up the ass-licking ranks."

Hirschman took a huge bite out of an Armenian cucumber, and said, "There's nothing like these bad boys. Dash of salt and pepper and they're a meal in themselves, so satisfying, especially fresh out of the fridge on a hot summer day. Come to think of it," Hirschman said, switching back to his original track, "to really get those prizes and publications these days you need a PhD. To be a Master in ass-licking isn't enough. Now you must be a Doctor at it. It doesn't hurt, naturally, that you're an ass-licking circus freak. Being Jew or Gay or Latino or African American or Native American or some dispirited person from Palestine or East Asia was enough to get you consideration for tenure not too long ago, but nowadays you have to be half goat, some identity in between make believe and reality: you have to be in some way uniquely and permanently hobbled, essentially beyond medical remedy. Verily, to secure a university position these days you have to be the human sort Jesus might've paused to cure on his way to Calvary."

Hirschman poured himself another slightly chilled glass of wine made from local barbera grapes, nicely acidic and fruity, and said, "But why should we stop here, since we're on a roll, because trailing this jubilee of convalescents are a host of equally decrepit critics and reviewers and literary talk show hosts whose only goal is cozying up to this or that publisher or agent—whom they will naturally need when they write their own magnum opus—or securing invitations to this dinner party and that awards ceremony where like any number of old garrulous generals defending some far-flung outpost they can opine for why their function is still indispensible, even if everyone outside the ridiculous gala has conceded that the empire has all but crumbled." Hirschman laughed at his own phrasing. "The worst of the worst of the old garrulous generals is this radio literary talk show sham located right here in LA," he said. (It took me a beat to register, we weren't in LA any longer.) "This once-upon-a-time serious reader has turned into an overfed book sow with his big pregnant pauses and oily-creepy, full-of-existential-wondering voice dripping with earnestness to the point of embarrassment. He is the sickliest sort of ass-licking seductress, a cheap stinky trick that, what the hell, you might as well fuck since he's a spit away and has his fat ass stuck up in the air. All these oppressed, repressed, suppressed, and most of all depressed—in sum, most so-called literary fiction writers—all waiting to get their turn at fat boy's anemic teats."

Finished with the lunch, Hirschman lit a cigarette, took a few puffs, and said, "The sow of pity lies in a bed of shit as the piglets fight for who is most pitiable and who among them should get first dibs, all the while the jolly oligarchs are running off with the farm. Bottom line: Forestiere, the joyful human gopher, was himself buried by these human farces, though in truth those who buried him in actuality, and not just metaphorically, were greedy commoners, simple street sharks, the kind that would've used Guernica to shade their porches in a pinch. Naw, Forestiere's body had barely turned cold when his siblings who inherited his estate began backfilling the gardens to create a stable subsurface suitable for commercial use. Only one of his brothers recognized his genius, and so what you see today is just a fraction of what Forestiere dug and shaped. The rest of the land was filled in and sold for the price of a parking lot and some of it was actually turned into one. *Can you imagine?* (In fact, never having been there myself, I could only imagine.)

"I can't wait to see it, " I told him.

He said, "Because they had a little slippage of earth recently it's down for repairs. In any case, minus that one brother, Forestiere's gardens were no more or less than holes that needed to be filled, and that's the fate, let's face it, of thousands of artists of this sort through the course of history. Any art that is about making oneself more at home in the world, especially in a way few, if any, have ever dreamed of making a home, all such art is automatically considered a hole, if not a shithole, that should be back-filled once the maker is dead and, if feasible, before. Forestiere took this massive pile of clay and began sculpting (as the first sculptors sculpted) from the inside out so that the earth might hold his body, sate his hunger, and pleasure his soul. What a difference from what we have today: Architecture that perplexes the body, famishes the appetite, and mortifies the soul. How about some dessert?" Hirschman left for the kitchen and returned with a couple of peaches, yellow skinned, super fuzzy, and the size of softballs. "You'll never taste anything like these lovelies. They've pushed all but a few of these trees. The farmer who gave them to me claimed in the old days they were used for canning." With a knife, he deftly cut the peach end to end and turned the halves in opposite directions until they popped apart and then gave me the half that didn't have the pit. The thick skin and fuzz was a lovely surprise to my teeth, but nothing compared to the super creamy flesh, extravagantly rich flavor, and the flood of juice now running down my fingers. "Ever taste anything like that?"

Before I could answer, he went on, "No, every artist in America should quiet down and visit, if not study The Gardens for a good long spell, especially architects. Not to say we should all take up his methodology and begin digging underground—though that wouldn't be such a bad idea—but that we should study his mind set, what he was after, what it meant." Hirschman had always been super fascinated by architecture and the meaning it harbored for a culture but it wasn't until then that he realized the importance of its very name: Arche (the first) + tect (maker). Architecture points to the first function, and, indeed, the inner essence of art: to make humans feel more at home in the world. Hirschman said, "But the oligarchs have taken the making of home away from us and left us only to *decorate* the home—with our megalomaniacal egos as the decorators. Bottom line: the world has become a palace of production and consumption and art exists for no other reason than to decorate that palace. All of so-called contemporary LA architecture is nothing more than decoration, decorative disasters, and, in most cases, so turned in on the architect's ego that it threatens to collapse from the incredible and sheer unipolar weight of it. The work of some architects, like that hook-nosed, carcass-feeding vulture whose work was smartly cordoned off to the West Side, thank god, is disaster alone, not even managing to rise to the level of decoration."

"Let's say it like it is, for how indifferent, even belligerent they are from everything that might matter to humans, for how ill-suited they are for squaring the human heart and soul and body with its living and resting and dying place, the most celebrated buildings of the last thirty years might as well be visually curious torture implements: Brazen Bulls, or Spanish Donkeys, or—better yet, and most apropos—Virgins of Nuremberg. There are so few exceptions to this rule they are barely worth mentioning. Drop a simple human mind anywhere in the so-called *new downtown* and within half an hour you will find it pulverized. Never before has human civilization seen such a wholesale capitulation to the avarice of the oligarchs as downtown LA; a soul-battering collection of super-scaled EGOs, one after another concrete and steel and asphalt misadventure seated amidst a street level conundrum calculated to keep the soul from coming to rest at any cost, a virtual Ho Chi Minh trail of vertical and horizontal, rails and barrels, *do this* and *don't do that* signs…and accompanying fines, and up and down and zig and zag and over and underground—all of it enough to make a gerbil scream uncle! Using the age-old ploy of *the more 'artistic' the clutter, the longer it will take for the innocents to become conscious of its actual monstrosity*, they confected Grand Park, a multi-tiered Judas Chair that even lost possums from horror won't approach."

For Forestiere, it was all tied to the simple need to make a home for himself and escape the summer heat; the vision/drive came of the exigencies of the *terroir*, as they call it, not the exigencies of an ego that fits every terrifying description of a magnetar. Forestiere's fearsome human solitude, the man's mind and vision perfectly plumb with his physical person—this is what was necessary to tunnel through to beauty, and the most sincere of beauties he had in fact tunneled through to— this is what drove Hirschman to the brink. He'd done nothing with his writing life approaching what Forestiere had done with his digging life, and this was not simply because he was a writer and Forestiere was a master builder, or rather, master digger.

As he drove away from Forestiere's that day, "*Vain, Vain, Vain,*" he kept repeating to himself, just like that, in threes until, south of Fresno, in a place called Selma, he saw a sign—**FARM FRESH STRAWBERRIES**—and pulled off the freeway. A quarter mile or so down the road, he rolled up to a shack behind which lay a field of strawberries where four people with wide straw hats were bent over harvesting, like a painting of Millet. The unexpected nineteenth century agrarian innocence of the scene settled his soul some. A girl, maybe twelve or thirteen, whom he initially took as Thai, was sorting berries behind a counter. There was dust in her hair, and her skin was blotched like desert camouflage, and her lips were too stern, Hirschman felt, for someone so young.

"How much for these beautiful strawberries?"

"Four dollars a basket or three for ten."

"That's a pretty good deal," he said.

"Would you like a basket?"

"Is that your family picking out there?" he wanted to know.

"Yes."

"Are they organic?" he asked. "The strawberries. Do you use pesticides?"

"When we have to, " she said, "or else they will rot in the field."

In his stupid city brain, strawberries were produced, not even farmed, by industrial strawberry conglomerates that rained chemicals on their fields when so much as a gnat showed up, and so he felt embarrassed for even having brought it up to this girl whose family was obviously there to make a simple living. He paid for a couple of baskets and asked if there was a place he could wash them and she gestured for him to come around the stand where she held them under the spigot of a five gallon water drum, most likely the family's drinking water. She gave him the strawberries and wiped her hands dry on her apron.

"I never realized it was so beautiful here," he said. She looked at him puzzled, and kind of giggled. "You don't think so?"

"No," she said. "Where are you from?"

He told her LA, and she said she'd like to go someday. "You've never been?"

"I've never been nowhere but here. We went to San Francisco one day to pick up my uncle who was coming to America, but came back right away and I don't remembering anything. It's so boring here. Every day and every thing is always the same. Brown and green is all you see. Wherever you look. I want to go to Los Angeles and see some beautiful buildings, and movie stars, and Disneyland, and cool clothes."

He asked her nationality, and she said, "Hmong," which he later learned was a tribal hill people from Laos, tens of thousands that had migrated to the valley in the eighties. He walked back to his car and sat on the hood. The sun had set and clouds, the color of bruises, migrated slowly across a blazing backdrop of blue and orange and pink. Almost to test himself, he tried to put into words what he was watching unfold out there, but there was no describing it; not only because its scale was so great, but because it kept changing, in color and form. Only you might say it was like being a spectator to the mind of God enjoying its pure perfection and play. As he sat there eating those strawberries and studying it, the sky, the mind of God, studying his own mind, filled with his challenging thoughts about Forestiere, he knew at once that San Francisco and its soft swooping hills all preciously quieted and gray with fog offered him nothing. He knew that he wasn't just going to Frisco to get away, but was going there to see if he might build a home there, and that if that were the case that inside of a few months he'd most certainly feel what he'd felt in LA, because until he built a home like Forestiere built a home, not just physically but spiritually, he would be churning in place, and so he decided to stay the night in Fresno.

He checked into a seedy motel right off the 99 and drove willy-nilly out in the country the whole of the next day, passing one vineyard and orchard and row crop after another, so deep and so many and so endlessly it was as though he'd segued into a parallel world with no way out; not that if he were ever stuck there he would've cared to exit because mile after endless mile of that lush horizontality was affecting him like a hypnotic, so much so that at one point he seriously considered pulling over and settling beneath a tree or vine for a nap, even though it hadn't hit noon and he'd had an exceptional nights sleep. He realized how much he enjoyed getting lost, and how he'd evidently stopped feeling that way and had become acclimated to not feeling that way, because driving down those country roads the lovely feeling of getting lost came back to him, filling him with what he could only describe as joy. Of course he was familiar with LA in a way that he was not familiar with the country, but still one should be

able to get lost in a city like LA, not just geograph-
ically but lost to oneself, because the opportunity
to get lost to oneself above and beyond anything
else is the opportunity to find oneself, as there is
no greater creative spur than concealment, the
self turned back upon itself with little more than
its own dreams and visions and torments to get
acquainted with.

"There are plenty of places to get distracted
from yourself in LA but no longer any place you
can get lost," Hirschman said, "and get lost in a
way that you know you'll eventually find your way
home. Instead, everywhere we turn we are faced
with the same sickening roundabouts, forever
familiar returns to what we imagine we are, and
what we believe we believe, a feeling that is not so
much familiar, in the sense that family is familiar,
but rather familiar in the sense that the lever, and
the candy that drops out when we hit it is familiar.
Mystery has been leached from anything in the
vicinity of LA. The only mystery that survives in
LA is the mystery of the mind, the mystery of its
enduring unhappiness amidst such remorseless
splendor. And to solve this mystery," Hirschman
added, "a thousand medicines and potions and
philosophies and spiritual exercises have gotten
concocted, most of which can only be described

as placebos at best and voodoo at worst. Culture is now nothing more than a more and more dazzling roundabout with no exit out where we can hit the familiar lever and have a familiar bonbon drop out. The oligarchs have discovered that no matter how ruthless and ridiculous the no exit roundabouts, people will enthusiastically follow so long as there is a familiar and regular lever to hit and a familiar bonbon drops out. The entire country has turned at once spiritually emaciated and physically obese, consuming nothing but such bonbons. All anybody wants anymore is confirmation of their confabulations, confirmation of what they already believe, and believe they are, and society now has a billion ways of confirming all of it, leaving any dialectic unthinkable without sending the brain that turns on this twisted axis of nothingness into a free fall, if not death spiral. It used to be the crazies would be forced to sit with their confabulations until they turned untenable or into sheer poison, but now they simply hit a link and—*voila!*—crazies world wide, with the very same confabulations, pop up in a nanosecond, bonbons dropping out in buckets. It used to be only the mentally corked and emotionally hobbled joined cults, now everyone is a member of one or another and society has become nothing more than a cult wrestling match for supremacy and the title most absurd," Hirschman said. "From the number of bonbon machines placed at every conceivable and inconceivable curve and turn, revolutions of any force or momentum are unthinkable today; but even where revolution isn't the answer or possible, absent is faith in rational and reasonable discourse, the good will faith in another's point of view," Hirschman went on. "We have become blind and bitter rivals fighting over crumbs—the crumbling fighting over crumbs. In fact, we are nearing the point where knowledge and the search for truth, if not truth itself, has become a simple nuisance."

Rounding back toward the 99 he saw a cherry orchard red with ripe fruit. He always thought of cherries coming from Washington, but there they were hanging in the hundreds, if not thousands, from a tree, and so he pulled to the side of the dusty road and right beside his car rolled a pickup. The driver stopped eye-to-eye with him and said, "Color's about there."

Hirschman said, "Red as a cherry corvette!"

The man, had to be a farmer, laughed. They got to talking and Hirschman asked him what rent was for one of these little country homes and he said, "Why you ask?"

On a whim Hirschman said, "Thinking about moving to these parts. I'm looking to get lost."

The man said, "Got a place back of the orchard sittin' idle that'll do the trick."

Hirschman had been living there for over a year, and though it had been blazing hot during the day the nights cooled terrifically, and that first night, kicking back on his porch overlooking Hirschman's garden, and listening in on, it seemed, the orchard's rustling, he poured us homemade brew, a raisin mash moonshine, clear as water, with a hint of anise. Not only was it remarkably delicious, but also within the hour I discovered its effects were nearly hallucinogenic, the warmest and yet vivid drift away and at the same time *toward* the center of all that mattered between us as friends.

"Can you believe how long we've been on this here earth together," he said, "through the good and the bad, the thick and the thin of it. You're the only one that's come of the dozens that said they would. Some think I'm crazy, others think *how quaint*, and then there are those that feel sorry for me. The reason they're not visiting is the same reason people can't bring themselves to visit a friend in a hospital bed. They don't want to remember me this way. On my deathbed, they imagine."

"And yet other people," I told him, "feel that you've gone AWOL, or even committed a kind of treason."

"Yes, it's been a mighty long and winding road for me to end up here, of all places, you're right, but here I am, and I want to tell you how very much happy I am. It's a nice place to live, out in the country, close to Fresno. The people are easy-going and there's no traffic and everywhere you turn things are growing in abundance; all true, but most of all, it's a place where one can learn to quiet down because nobody is really looking at you, and nobody really cares what you do or don't do, so long, naturally, as you don't stir up trouble.

"That 'Vain, Vain, Vain' I blurted out when I left the gardens had to be taken seriously, and I ultimately decided it was nothing short of a mortal challenge. I felt I had no other option than to stop writing all together until I attained something akin to Forestiere's frame of mind." Until, he told me, he could actually achieve in writing something like Forestiere achieved in digging, but he had no idea at the time, and still had no idea, how that would happen, whether he would simply fail to write another word or tunnel through to the light. He told me he never realized the psychological terrorism that he'd been made to endure in LA, terrorism no doubt that was present in the Central Valley as well, if not across the globe, even to the remotest slums, "because, let's face it, humans first and foremost, above and beyond anything else, are psychological terrorists who wake in the morning only to consort with their ministers of intimidation and degradation and review or refresh or recalibrate their plans for psychologically terrorizing everyone around them that might in the least frustrate their aims." Still, he'd concluded, there are places where the terrorism is essentially infrastructural, fundamentally inexorable—places like LA.

"For years in LA," he said, "I had this strange feeling, what the old time French called *depaysement*, the feeling of being a foreigner, an outsider who pines for home, except I felt this way about the city I was born and raised in—strange. But maybe this is the way that writers feel no matter where they live. It used to be they'd escape to another country to finally recover their love for, or at least see it with fresh eyes, their home country, but now it seems no matter where you escape to you're escaping to the same place, so who knows? Maybe someday if I go so far as to do what Forestiere did, dig a hole and live in there forever, I'd still feel the same. Maybe it's no longer possible to make a home, only decorate it."

We kept the moonshine pouring, and had near about plowed through half the quart, when I looked up from Hirschman's confession, and critique, and noticed the thinnest east-travelling clouds blowing swiftly across the moon.

"As much as these farmers need rain, at this time of year it would probably be a disaster," I said.

"A little just wets down the avenues and knocks off the dust," Hirschman said, "you're right, a day or two of straight rain and all hell breaks loose in the fields. But everyone is praying that once this harvest ends the rain will come, because if it doesn't, no one knows whether this great experiment in agriculture, one of the greatest humans have ever known, will survive."

Returning to his writing, Hirschman told me that should he fail to write another word both terrorized him and liberated him, because he realized immediately that what he imagined he had built up in terms of himself was enmeshed with what he had written, and that should he not write another word he might unravel; but then again, the very thought that his psychology depended upon writing also terrorized him, as no human should depend upon art to make him whole, because his life, every living, breathing moment of it, is his ART: art as practice, art as a way of going in the world, art as the crafting of a hearth, even to the hour of death when the hearth finally swallows you up. *Waiting for Lipchitz at Chateau Marmont*, I thought. LA killed Hirschman because it did not provide for him—one of the city's most faithful stewards—a means of crafting a hearth. He'd left to craft a hearth in the Central Valley and had died trying.

That night we talked in a way that we could never talk in LA, until just past 2:00 a.m., when I retired to his spare bedroom with a single mattress on the floor. I opened the window and turned off the light and laid there listening to the crickets and wind, waiting, ritualistically for the insomnia to rear its head. I had the Ativan and Ambien and I had the Oxycodone and Oxycontin, and even some time-released morphine, not to mention Xanax and Klonipin. I had the gamut from calming to knock-out pharmaceuticals, either bought or in some cases pilfered—if you consider pilfering taking from your dying mother who obviously will have no use for all of it, since the cancer was advancing more swiftly than her pill count was dwindling. As a matter of course, I'd try one, and if that didn't work, I'd try another. If that didn't work, I'd go for two or three in combination. It was all in my duffel next to the mattress, but rather than taking one, or a combination, I found my thoughts drifting back to times gone by, to Hirschman, and I lounged on the balcony of my dazzling house-on-stilts, sipping the smallest of small batch Kentucky bourbon or Irish whiskey, toasting to his recent novel or my recent script, and thanking our lucky stars that we had this city and that we had each other from forever as friends. But also how the guilt would sneak in once he'd leave, and I'd find myself struggling to justify my highflying lifestyle with his tiny one bedroom–flat-lifestyle, in Koreatown, above a gaudy furniture store, and across the hall from a nut job that believed the government was eyeing his every keystroke. Even so, I'd tell myself, Hirschman is rich in freedom. He wrote what he wanted to write without compromise, without consideration of advances or royalties, or even critics, while from the start I had to compromise, often fighting for scenes and even lines, worried stiff about financing, and obliged to work with a so-called "team." On top of that, I'd tell myself, he might've had a place of his own if he'd taken some of his royalties, however modest, and invested in a small place in, say, Echo Park, rather than spent endlessly on an endless number of books, stacked to the rafters on every surface of his apartment, half of which he never even read. Remember those job offers from USC and Occidental? Both he'd turned down because he believed that for a writer to teach creative writing for a livelihood was a disaster, and because an artist must *live in the cracks.*

To level the scales, I piled it on until we were eye to eye, until what he *got* and where he *was* was exactly what he deserved, and, conversely, what *I* got and where *I* was was precisely what I deserved. Now, I was forced to admit that neither foolhardiness nor courage had brought Hirschman here, and neither was it that epiphany at Forestiere's, per se. No, it was his disciplined attentiveness to things both quotidian and profound, the high and low and in between, the million windows onto the world which he'd kept open even during the most terrible storms and blinding light; that state of mind, if not state of being, allowed the bird of insight to land on his shoulder. He'd always tuned into what mattered, while what mattered only mattered to me when matters pushed me to it, when every option had been exhausted and I had no other choice. This is probably why I hadn't revealed to Hirschman how far into the Hollywood gorge I'd actually fallen; this is why I'd been shamefully out of touch with him for months. The only thing I had going over Hirschman was my LA wealth and status, and I actually feared that Hirschman—with a bestseller or movie deal— would someday trump me on that front, too. I liked the status quo between us, and now, for the first time in decades, that status quo was up- ended. That was the truth: here was Hirschman trumping me, as it turned out, with one of the humblest cards in the deck. Just like Hirschman. *Touché my friend!* The blade went straight to my heart, the running blood purging, and with that concession to Hirschman's hard earned inner ge- nius, I fell fast asleep and stayed asleep only to waken sometime during the night to the beautiful sound of a train at some distance, hooting: *I am here and I am crossing and soon I will be gone.* It echoed the path of my life, the youthful rumbling, the growing roar, its slow ebbing, and, eventually, vanishing. I could just smell the rabbit jambalaya Hirschman had thrown together stewing every so slowly on the lowest possible flame in the back of his oven.

"In the morning, this will be wonderful," Hirschman said, before we both hit the sack.

I confess, my vanishing, just then, felt ravishing. "If Hirschman can do it, why can't I? I can die here," I said to myself. "I can die here content; I can die a nobody in the middle of nowhere California."

I had surrendered, the final stage of a yearlong struggle, very much like, I imagine, what one goes through when told one has a terminal illness. Waiting at the Chateau, it all came back to me, how, after coming to terms with my mortifying finances, I buttoned and scaled down, how the initial thought of moving away and joining the human monotony outside of LA crippled me with panic attacks. Relax, if not Los Angeles there was New York, or San Francisco, or even Seattle, though New York was the only city where one might be perceived as moving horizontally, at least as far as show business was concerned. But none of those cities was significantly less mercenarily expensive than Los Angeles, and so I jumped to a two bedroom in Silver Lake, before jumping to a one bedroom in Echo Park, before slinking into a miniscule and windowless basement studio in Mid-Wilshire, dark and foreboding a place as oceanographers are now discovering the most uncanny sea life thriving.

There was no question of inviting anyone over, and so my apartment now not only looked like a safe house, but effectively became one, and it was there, and only then I first seriously entertained "the conversation," and its endless iterations, in substance all equally retarded, amounting to how I could explain my exit of the city to the likes of Pacoima or Pomona *gracefully*, if that's the word: "Yeah, I'm not getting anything out the city anymore;" or, "It's a great place, sure, but the people moving here aren't committed Angelenos anymore;" or, "I just think I need a break." But no sooner had I begun these hypothetical conversations than they would end with the same damning and full-on factual comeback: "Would you stay here if you had a place paid for in full in the Palisades?" The reflexive answer was, "Of course the fuck yes," because what every Angeleno took for granted was that the city was a hundred different cities, and the LA you were complaining about might be a different and fabulous LA just fifteen minutes away, the LA your next deal, needless to say, would land you in flush with cash.

Everyone in LA when they *made it* dreamed of a 4,000-ish square-foot place with a good-size backyard where they'd plant their own garden or even raise their own chickens. In fact, countless numbers of people dreamed of graduating from their one bedroom to a small estate where they could slow down and exit the asphalt and feel the grass beneath their feet and save the whales and watch those great old silent movies in repose. But short of reaching their astral aims, deposit those same approaching absolute zero people to an earthly estate far out in the country in, say Temecula, or Chino, (much less Fresno!), and they would whither from loneliness and despair, as they could only brook living there so long as their image was projected elsewhere, in fact, everywhere. Waiting for Lipchitz at the Chateau, I was struck by the monstrous irony that people from all over the world dream of fleeing their homes for LA, while people from LA dream of fleeing their homes for these other people's towns and homes—vacated, naturally, of all those people and left to return to kind of vegan sanctuary with shamans on call and llamas roaming contentedly. Whole societies are now caught in this purgatory of *neither at home here* nor *at home there,* exiting where they are for a place that isn't what they dream it is, and consequently abandoning for rot their haven and (in Hirschman's memory) their hearth (if the entirety of my current accounting isn't in Hirschman's memory) and the warmth it gives: all of it abandoned for the dreamy gaseous light of the magic lantern. The sheer image of friends' faces—discounting, shocked, flat-out disbelieving—when I broke the news that I had to leave, followed by their excruciating *here, here, it'll all be all right* pity was unbearable.

Traffic, smog, the bottomless and ravenous egos, I enumerated all of the obvious, true as they ever were, but much less true, and even much less obvious, than that I was flat broke with no skills other than writing in a day and age when writing is as marketable as those doilies knitted by grandma. If only I had made this decision or another decision, if only I'd stayed in touch with so-and-so and called him for lunch every once in a while. I flogged myself until the skin broke. That's when I finally confronted my agent, who, from fear of losing I'd made a million excuses for.

Her office was beautiful as usual with floor to ceiling windows, just as beautiful as the first day I'd stepped into it when she told me that the one thing that would set her apart from other agents was her devotion to her writers even in troubled times; the other thing that set her apart from all the rest was her belief not only in the material but in the person: "You're different," she said; "you're an artist," she said. "Writer's come and go and, honestly, are a dime a dozen, but there are very few *artists* among the tens of thousands of writers in this city, and this is what makes us a perfect match." She did her bachelor's in literature at Harvard and an MBA at Columbia, and even though I'd been briefed by three other writers that she was a pitiless negotiator, I just then believed that in her heart of hearts she was a bookish coed reading Coleridge and travelling by VW van all the way to Ashland just to see *The Tempest*. I'd never felt so believed in, so loved, and loved at the one thing that I truly and deeply loved and wanted to be loved for: writing. She was nearly middle-aged and not particularly attractive, but I'd have fucked her right there on her massive glass desk to give you a sense of how perfectly I was smitten. When I walked through the door she was busy at her desk, beside her floor-to-ceiling glass windows, and I thought: *how ironic that that this should be the architectural detail of choice for a world that was so cold-bloodedly opaque.* She waited for a good ten seconds before looking up, and then came to with a big smile, as though she'd just landed a 767 size contract for me, rather than failed to land even a balsa wood glider for the past five years. She was wearing a black blouse and black pants and her black hair was pulled back, and her eyes were black, too, her whole aspect dead set against joy and color, as though she were a paid bearer of the cruelest news.

And to stay with the image, "How have you been?" she asked, as though I'd recently lost my girlfriend and she hadn't even managed to send a card.

"Not so good," I told her, precisely what she expected me to say, as on cue she proceeded to tell my why I was feeling *not so good*, and yes, she said it just like that, *let me tell you why you're feeling not so good*, with the emphasis in elaboration falling quietly hammer-like on the *industry right now*, a statement there was no contesting on the one hand and absolutely meaningless on the other, because everyone knew there was no such thing as *the industry*. Other than a few jackasses thumbing through scripts, until one jackass got hyped up about it and sent it up to the next jackass who got hyped up about it, and so on. Her condescension, part and parcel of her personality, was precisely what my ire/frustration needed to unbridle, and the very moment it did unbridle was also the very moment she was deciding the precise implements she'd use to put the nag whining from across her desk down for good. My point of view, I suppose, was general among writers having fallen out of grace for such an embarrassingly long spell—*get off your ass, bitch!* After stamping on her black-haired head for ten minutes or so—*you promised me this, you told me that*—I eased up and vowed that my next script would be tailored to hit the G-spots of every producer in town; as a concession to her and, naturally, survival for myself. "Here it is," I said, laying *Homer All Alone* delicately on her immense glass desk.

In the face of the tidal waves of imbecility crashing against our industry's shores, I had decided to go with the flow, learn the rip tide's art of misdirection and seduction. I decided to tell my tale in such a way that the politburo would find crazy funny, tickle the belly, rather than rattle the soul. In an age when all the people want is reprieve from their nine-to-five grind, this is what great artists do, I told myself. Still, walking away from that meeting, I was forced to ask whether all my reporting and, later, screenwriting, about corruption and injuries and injustices, systemic and otherwise, had merely been a way of reporting on corruptions and injuries and injustices, systemic and otherwise, that had afflicted me, and that once the going got rough I was just as happy to turn away from these principles and fly headlong into the lantern's hypnotic light. For years I believed I was too roiled by memory and injustice to frolic on the surface, too romantic to dance with the Hollywood mannequins, and then there I was, with this ridiculous script looking for a return ticket to the dazzling Deadman's Ball. The hearty yuk-yuks *Homer* elicited from my NEW agent, the *It's terrific and I think I can do something with this*, made me ask why I'd taken so long to get rid of that glass-house bitch, but one week passed, then a month, then two, and from *I think I can do something with this*, to *I'm not getting the response I hoped for* to *I've caught wind that maybe something similar is already in the cutting room*, to *The situation is very dynamic in the industry right now*, causing me to sink deeper and deeper into self-despair. Now, Lipchitz, one of the most serious producers in the city, was interested in my recent script, hardly a comedy. Yes, it had taken him nine months to get back to me, but that he wanted to meet was not something someone like Lipchitz would ask to do if he hadn't something serious in mind; yes, from what you'd heard, he, too, had joined the ranks of sell-out artists trolling the city, but there was no question that he'd done good work in the past, even superior work, getting behind indies, two with cutting-edge gay themes, that were box office successes at a time when independent theatres were flourishing, when half a dozen movie houses in the city screened on any given night any number of films produced outside the Hollywood dialysis ward; when one could settle in for a couple of hours to watch stories unfold, stories not necessarily brilliant but at least interesting and crafted by an actual flesh-and-blood team of people rather than what is churned out today, a hundred different variations on robotic awfulness, the same cobbling together of the same old stories where the Mengelian prints of a dozen producers punish every page.

Sitting at the Chateau, waiting for Lipchitz, I now recalled my one and only meeting with him, at a dinner party thrown by a fellow writer at his Santa Monica condo just months after I sold my first script. There were seven of us, all up-and-comers in the industry, and Lipchitz, by strides, the most powerful player in the room. We'd been waiting for him through cocktail hour and were just about to sit for dinner when the doorbell rang and our hosts said, "It must be Saul," and went to fetch him. He was taller and thicker than I pictured, wearing khakis and, to hide his girth, I assumed, an unusually poufy blood-orange fleece sweater. When he approached I saw his baseball cap was Dodgers, and that his black beard petered in a surprisingly ugly way down his beefy neck.

The hosts, Jeff, my age, and his young boyfriend, whose name I forget, but barely drinking age, introduced Lipchitz, and to avoid our jockeying for the inside track, arranged us at the long farmer's table with Lipchitz seated in the middle. As they excused themselves to the kitchen, we all tried our best, without sounding desperate, to engage Lipchitz who seemed about as uninterested in us as we were interested in him, answering any number of perfectly innocuous questions, as in, "So, what have you been working on recently?" with "Few things here and there;" or, "I loved Point of Pleasure," with a rapid, "Good-good-good." A go-to retort, indeed, nearly a tic, I soon concluded, that he deployed like a tommy gun to eliminate whatever line of thought might chance spring to life: "Industry been treating you good, Saul?" with "Good-good-good."

Finally the food mercifully arrived. He brushed the vapors of the couscous to his nose and guessed: "Toasted in butter first? Bingo! And tossed with dried apricots and pine nuts, obviously; and the Brussels sprouts: roasted with shallots, olive oil, and balsamic, I imagine, and for that most gorgeous carmelization, what, for an hour at three-twenty-five?"

"You're good Saul, very good, but not flawless: An hour-and-a-half at three hundred, close!" He actually poked his fork, clean, but still, into the teak bowl to sample the radicchio and endive salad (fresh from the Santa Monica farmer's market) dressed, we learned from the boyfriend, in simple vinaigrette, as the pending feast was already quite rich. The kid wasn't kidding: they must've paid a small fortune for the main attraction, a massive blackish fish (barracuda, ridiculously, popped to mind) that they lugged in on an even more massive clay platter. Lipchitz presently fell upon this leviathan like a long lost friend, asking one after another question about its tortuous sojourn to our table. Whatever direction the biggest gun in the room wants to take the conversation is where the conversation enthusiastically goes, so there we were for minutes on end with Jeff explaining they'd trudged all the way to San Pedro to fetch this stunning creature, a local sea bass, as it turned out.

"What kind of *sea bass*?" Lipchitz wanted to know (*sea bass* had become the catchall name for any number of unidentifiable fish, he claimed). Our hosts couldn't say for sure, though their monger in San Pedro vouched for its sweet tasty oiliness, an omega-3 bomb.

Moving ahead, we were elucidated on the coarseness and source of the Malaysian curing salt, and on the temp and time that turned the fish's skin so deliciously crinkled and crusty, and on the charred twiggy things crisscrossing its flank: rosemary and dill. The boyfriend had "borrowed" the recipe from *Michael's*, where he'd worked for a spell (at that age doing who-knows-what besides washing dishes). And did Lipchitz smell lemon emanating from its copious cavity? "Yes, and I have to brag here, the olive oil we finished it with is from a grove in Tuscany that we own shares in."

Actually," Jeff put in, "three trees we adopted three years ago."

Such was Lipchitz' curiosity of that fish's preparation and pedigree, you'd think it were an emanation from some crucible of oceanic mystery—whereon I began to feel the most sick and paradoxical jealousy of it, paradoxical because for all the veneration it was getting, suddenly lying there on that platter, in all its black twiglet covered fleshiness, it brought to mind a napalm victim of some remote jungle conflict. So much so that when Jeff conveyed chunks of it to our plates with his massive tongs I felt I might throw up. In contrast, Lipchitz, who manifestly resembled a bear, was soon eating like one, too, at the banks of a river, chomping and slurping until food spittle materialized at the sides of his mouth, the animalism of his appetite scandalous if he weren't utterly inoculated by talent and fame. At one point, reaching across the table for yet another bottle of Beaujolais (by my estimate he'd guzzled through just short of two) *that paired fabulously with the fish,* he caught an oily sprig of rosemary on the furry sleeve of his poufy sweater. Like he'd just come in from a roll in the grass, there it adhered while he filled his wine glass, big enough for a few smaller fish to swim in, to the brim. It was then, too, that I noticed a sliver of nail polish on the cuticles of the index and middle fingers of his right hand, and I wondered, out of sheer frustration with him, I suppose, the small feminine under part his big body played in some gay sexcapade the night before.

We'd just about finished dessert, a fresh berry tart with stunningly rich custard, when Lipchitz, sated and undoubtedly sloshed, perused the room and tapped the table rhythmically with his fork; his countdown to departure, I thought, when he dropped the fork, removed his Dodgers cap, and

with his big bushy fingers scratched his scalp vig-
orously, to get his brain moving again, as it turned
out, because the second he slapped the cap back
on he launched us into a most serious discussion
about film, asking and listening and moving the
conversation around for what had to be an hour,
as though he were conducting a master class, and
not just so that he'd have a platform to blab, what
I guessed would be the case. "What are people
looking for in films these days?" he asked. "Do
we give them what they want or what they need?
Should film reflect the culture or critique it, or do
the best films do both, or should our goal be simple entertainment? If you had to choose between
making one film that would change the world but
leave you broke, or a dozen decent enough films
that would land you in St. Moritz twice a year,
which would it be? Films surpassed book, books
surpassed bards, and bards surpassed chants, and
chants surpassed grunts and groans and gurgling,
I imagine. So what will surpass film in the future?
Something will? No?"

On this one, everyone took a turn, holograms
and 3D, and sundry beta-level technologies, and
eventually I did too: "If we continue to make films
the way we're making them, anything and everything will surpass us. But if we make films that

unearth the human situation in all its complexity, then nothing will. Film at its best is unsurpassable because reality is unsurpassable," I, the youngish screenwriter, full of faith and shit in equal measure, said.

Lipchitz chuckled kindly, and said, "Heroic," and after another go around the table, quit the conversation just as suddenly as he started it. Yes, how determined I was to make a mark, and how he must've been just as determined with wildly original movies like *Queer Face*, and *Spilling Over the Waves*; yet in the long run how even more determined the industry would be to prove us wrong. Even ten years ago what might've started out as a tidy script with a couple of smart twists tinkered with by a producer or two, has now become the monster product of a dozen dysfunctional minds that, by the time their doctoring is done, has turned that script into a retarded yarn vacant of any function other than to discombobulate surely as would the most whacked-out roller coaster ride; leaving you with a strange exhilaration and vague nausea, a kind of sick wonderment, say, that something like that had been done to you and that you had actually enjoyed it. All the serious writers are disgusted by it but nobody is saying anything about it because to say is tantamount to becoming your own Dr. Kevorkian. No, there must be absolute agreement, even an occult suicidal pact, that what is being produced by— let's return to calling them Mengeles—is absolutely appropriate to and required of our times and absolutely what the people need and want and, above and beyond anything else, absolutely what *Der Filmmaker* deems necessary for survival. We have been decimated and humiliated, our territory chipped away at and our currency devalued, and we must now use everything, including every idiocy in our vast idiocy arsenal, to eliminate the threat. If occasionally we make a movie or show that seems to teach, preach, or steward, let it be, as in the Beatles, but do not become distracted from those highfalutin occasionals into believing that is why we are here, and that is what we are made to do. Do not be fooled or grow haughty, even if these films are awarded a statue or two, and, in fact, please sit down, in fact we quite intentionally hand these films a statue or two on the so-called world stage so that we might continue making films vacant of virtue all the more remorselessly. We are strictly here to feed the lantern that feeds us and to which we are indebted, and to which the entire world is indebted, because its light has done more to help defeat darkness and boredom than anything else in one hundred years.

Sitting at the Chateau, waiting for Lipchitz, I recall Hirschman once saying, "The festering of boredom at the bottom of the human soul may be the only existential truth left to fully fathom." Yes, the fear of boredom is today what the fear of lust was for centuries among the most merciless enforcers of the Catholic Church. Everything is oriented toward thwarting its passage into the human soul for dread of the most destructive evil gaining root and, at the same time, all of Hollywood's energies are concerted to proliferate boredom at every turn; for without boredom, Hollywood's function would entirely cease to exist. Let's say that the fear of boredom is one chamber of the Hollywood heart and the proliferation of boredom the other, the two chambers pumping in perfect coordination. Outside of boredom and its festering pustulating [sic] reality at the human soul's core there is basically no existential truth that has not already been brought into the light of day or shuttled into a museum and placed upon a pedestal to instruct all of humanity, only to be visited by a few octogenarians and twittering school kids bussed in from around the district—(Hirschman). There was a time when the goal was to bring what was hidden in the shadows out of the shadows and into the light, but what we see now is light radiating on nearly every existential truth and humans reaching for their big dome all-weather umbrellas for cover—(Hirschman). Ultimately, let's face it, the human truth is also boring; after coming to terms with the human truth, humans must still escape the monotony of the human condition—(Hirschman).

There was a time, of course, when one could earn a decent living and sleep well at night knowing that having whored oneself out might've been a bit distasteful, but what with the lifestyle it afforded—a nice 2,500 square-foot home in Brentwood or the Hills + Audi A6 or tricked out Prius + two or three trips to NY a year + a month long European vacation every other—all this still made whoring a persuasive proposition. But it all fell to pieces once we started contesting the pimp's cut. We took to the streets bitching and moaning about their avarice, but as we bitched and blathered we blinkered ourselves from the streetwalkers that were taking over every corner. And there were far more corners than we ever imagined, stretching from Vancouver to the north and New Orleans to the south, and that compared to what we charged, for pennies on the dollar, in cars, in telephone booths, or motels that rented mattresses by the hour, they turned pretty decent tricks. My friends in TV, especially, couldn't fathom a world without themselves because they hadn't fathomed that their work had sunk to the lowest common denominator, and once it had reached the lowest common denominator, the lowest common denominator could do the work practically anywhere and for themselves! To put it yet another way: they had brought, or been made to bring reality, to an ant's point of view, and then the ants started swarming. By the time they looked up, these living tidbits were eating them alive. In the end, actually, the whole affair better compared to an old-fashioned farming operation: the networks and studios were doing to us what any peach farmer does to a tree to up his profits/ production—ruthlessly prune so that when, from its winter slumber, the tree wakes, it panics, and starts pushing out a surplus of shoots and buds in an automatic impulse to propagate and survive. I had learned this farming fact from Hirschman, one of a handful of farming facts that I just knew even as I was acquiring them that I would keep for the rest of my life, as they were not just facts of farming but facts for living. "You have to know when to stress your plants. Give them too much

love and they hold back their fruit, but stress them
too much and they give up and die. If the land
is packed too tight, you have to rip it, sometimes
over and over, before plugging in the tree. Across
the board, the sweetest fruit is always marked by a
pit or bruise or scar."

On my second day visiting Fresno, I chanced
upon my apartment just off the Fulton Mall,
which, as it turned out, was yet another cultural landmark in that part of the valley, and one
that Hirschman discovered a few months into
his *self-exile* (what I called it, not Hirschman).
He was lunching at the Chicken Pie Shop in the
Tower District when he spotted an article in the
local progressive newspaper about city hall's de-
bate to tear up an outdoor mall, whose boosters
claimed was a national treasure. He didn't know
what to expect of this Fulton Mall, but within a
week he'd visited it twice for three hours and was
soon fully conversant of its history, and as we
drove there that afternoon, he filled me in. Before
its construction the Fulton Mall had been Fulton
Street, a vital downtown shopping hub with a rich
history, where, for instance, the young William
Saroyan used to peddle newspapers. But by the
mid-sixties, Fresnans began forsaking it in favor

of a new and flashy and temperature-controlled indoor mall, located a few miles north.

To stave this exodus, and protect the city's core, a well-known Austrian architect, Victor Gruen, was brought on board. Alongside landscape architect Garrett Eckbo. Fulton Street and the blocks adjacent were reimagined as a vast outdoor mall with cars shunted to the margins—where we now parked and proceeded on foot—that would wed all the exigencies of shopping with the quiet contentment of strolling a public park. I was immediately enchanted by the mall's intelligent playfulness; the concrete was imbedded with curving metal bands that suggested the winding way of a river, and one after another, block after block, the most imaginative water fountains, in bronze or ceramic tiled, fantastical geomorphic sculptures, and small pools came into view. There were occasional places of stillness, where you could sit on a bench, some street level and some up a small flight of stairs, and take in the dappled light falling through the many handsome and fully mature trees. Hirschman and its boosters weren't exaggerating: it was a work of genius, an architectural and landscape gem in the middle of nowhere, and at first Fresnans came in adoring droves, Hirschman told me.

You could purchase shoes or a coat and then rest on a bench beside a burbling sculptural waterfall and enjoy, since they were *Valley Boys*, Steinbeck, or Saroyan, the latter, who was "one of the best writers of the twentieth century, but whose work, not to mention memory, has been buried because he wasn't cynical enough, wasn't arse-kissing of the critics enough," so Hirschman claimed. "Anyway, it worked for a while, but when another indoor mall even further fucking north was built, there was yet another hegira. After that, the only regular visitors were the old timers; Armenians and Italians and Chinese and Japanese and probably some Jews, too, because there were quite a few Jewish merchants here from my research. They would while away the hours playing pinochle or backgammon or chess and sharing, quite literally, war stories, one imagines; but they were there mostly to socialize, and so one by one the stores closed, and for at least thirty years the mall had been all but abandoned." *All but*, because interspersed between the stately boarded up buildings were venders selling Chinese made flea market sundries, blinking light toys, and cheap Teflon pans, and fall-apart socks by the dozen, as well as a handful of hipper establishments bravely trying to make a go of it amidst the chintz.

"You will find here," he said, nodding to half a dozen kids playing on the mall, "sadness, hopelessness, loneliness—of the negative emotions— you will find the human reflexes to the human condition, existential reactions to existential conditions, but hardly a trace of the LA mind, one that makes an utter mess of itself trying to square its insane image of what it wants to be and believes it is entitled to be with what it actually is. But, maybe the LA mind, like everything else it touches or ponders for any length of time, is going global, too. It is," he said, "a national, if not worldwide, fiasco."

I thought to myself, *it might very well be*, but I was falling for the mall and just then what might happen to the world-at-large seemed a simple hypothetical next to its playful concrete reality, where I began to feel a kind of depressurization and let my mind wander rather than anticipate disaster, and my body relax rather than brace for frustration. So far from home, I felt the most satisfying sense of safety and even more of anonymity, if not invisibility. After walking the length of it a couple of times, we slipped into a relatively new beer joint, all dark wood paneling with couches and a small stage for a band, and there, over three quite excellent IPAs, we discussed the mall and finally concluded that it was the fate of most great post-war urban projects, if not all of post-war urban life, and there seemed, anymore, no way to stop it. Did he consider the *Grove* something similar that *had* succeeded? And he answered, "Absolutely not" (not that he hadn't considered it): "The Fulton Mall's sculptures and squares and water fountains were meant to delight the eye and set the brain in play, and its many many sitting areas were there to give the people a place to ease up and reflect, while the *Grove* and its twin monstrosity in Glendale were simply there to corroborate the eye and sedate the brain and to keep people from coming to rest and reflection at any cost. And at the design level," Hirschman said, "that megalomaniac's small town, old style architecture, with Sinatra all piped in, and its sweet ding-a-ding-a-ding train running through the middle, is a return to the past, not in order to claim the triumphs of the past, not in order to harness the energies of the people for future triumphs, however glorious or inglorious, but rather the past was there to act as a nostalgic vessel for the transit of goods, just as Marmont is a nostalgic vessel for the transit of goods, however much those goods are humans."

How ironic that I should recall this sitting there at Chateau Marmont, waiting for Lipchitz.

"It used to be the city was where commerce, culture, geography, and history all fused into home, but now only commerce has survived, indeed feasting on the carcasses of the others, in all its radical free-floating actuality," Hirschman said. "Everything now has been subsumed under commerce, including, let's face it, so-called high art, that is now nothing more than a vast transient window display. Even The Rock at LACMA is a vast transient window display, one that hoped to be so much more, but came too late upon the scene to make any difference, no matter how big or whatever wheeler the truck hauling it on its back was, because it turned light as a balloon the minute it was situated on that preposterous site. Mass and grounding, going under and digging beneath, and being all quieted down there—all of it is over, all show, theatrics, what the museum, itself an edifice, or maybe sarcophagus for the embalming of egos and institutionalizing of dough, plainly attests to. Like these Egyptian pharaohs, a place for the dead to promulgate their presence into eternity, only gutted of the spiritual, even if eternity itself depends upon the spiritual to give it any bite—that's what LACMA is, and that's what culture is, and that's precisely what Angelenos in their essence are. They claim they are spiritual without being at all religious, when, in fact, the precise opposite is true: they are religious without being in the least spiritual. Without, of course, ever admitting the word God or the like, they adhere to all of religion's irrationalities: wishful thinking, faith in half facts, and full-on fantasies, including veneration of the most ludicrous idols, but without any spiritual force working to hold the preposterousness up from within. They want it to disappear," Hirschman said, changing direction, again, as was his custom.

"What do you mean *who wants what to disappear?*"

"The mall," he said. "Way I told you, they were debating the issue, but now, it appears, the deal is all but done. They're going to rip it out and run a road through it. The same way they've run a road right through everything and anything that matters anymore."

"Who is doing this?"

"Naturally," he said, "developers from Los Angeles are leading the charge. They've run out, I assume, of places to desiccate in LA, so now they're moving their desiccating machines and logic here."

The mall was at the bottom of a mile long corridor known as the Arts District where a local developer had put up some nice-looking live-work spaces, as they call it, and so on our way out, definitely buzzed and still excoriating the LA developers and Fresno City Council sellouts that would allow the destruction of something so treasurable, we stopped to take a look. The apartments were modern in design, steel and smooth stucco and sparkling clean windows for lots of sun, and within walking distance of the mall. When the manager told us the price, which was near about a third of what you'd pay in LA for a similar flat, I almost saw drunken stars.

"Are you interested?" the manager asked.

"Naw," I said, when I came to. "Just curious."

I *was* curious, I discovered, as I drove home three days later, past Selma and Kingsburg and Dinuba and Bakersfield, curious in a way that itself was curious, my soul struggling with Fresno, as though it were a concept, a stand-in for something beyond a city or place to live or not live; and the very fact that I was struggling, and not abjectly defeated, made me feel more alive than I'd felt in over a year. In particular, what had me in its spell, still, was the slumber I knew in that little room on that little mattress, the all embracing quiet, and the way I slipped into my dreams, and how the distant rumble and hoot of the train woke me almost like a mother checking to see if her child is sleeping tight. *Is this feeling what I feared?* I asked, during my three-and-a-half hour drive home. That wholesome slumber that is death's small dose. Did I fear that the life force upon moving to Fresno would reverse course, and transform into a slo-mo black hole, where who I was and what I dreamed of becoming would chunk by chunk diminish to pebble size anonymity, to sand and silt, a trailing chain of atoms, and finally to nothingness. Did I fear the very seduction of nothingness, the innate existential exhaustion that tugs on us from the start, and manifests in lethargy, laziness, self-destruction, and, most common of all, boredom.

Yes, I was afraid this would finally win my heart; the deep nearly carnal yearning to renounce life, and all its drives and appetites, for the interminable and insatiable march toward, to use two of Hirschman's favorite words, *dissolution* and *death.* By moving away I would suddenly announce my departure from the epic making of history and renounce my *maybe* future contribution to it. I would, above and beyond everything else, no longer be a thing of consequence, no longer be part of the exhilarating cosmic mix, the countless dice throws and random folds and endless paroxysms that brought this thing that goes by a thousand names into existence, however ultimately inconsequential. I would be an inconsequential amidst the inconsequential, rather than a consequential amidst the inconsequential. This is what my mother meant when she rattled on about the culture in LA. To be consequential, to be in the exhilarating mix, the exhilarations in her case almost irrelevant, however large or small, they would shake her axis the same: "You should've heard Placido tonight. I'm still trembling in my chair!" was just as likely as "You should have tried this new cupcake at Crumb. I'm still swimming in its tasty goodness!"

All this meant is that she had tasted the life force and swam away from death's vortex. But why should I fear it, when for the last year I'd dreamed of hardly anything but the vortex? I could choose anything now, any version of myself into the future, because, in a way, I had already chosen my own nothingness, and when one chooses one's own nothingness, if only in one's imagination in a concentrated way, the world opens up, and anything becomes an option, an option over nothing. Something, or rather, anything, or anyone, over nothing. I wanted to surrender all the infantile ego, all the go nowhere ego, even if I knew that there was no way to ultimately surrender it without surrendering the life force itself.

I had these thoughts all the way through the soft rolling hills of the Tehachapi's, through Magic Mountain, and by the time I reached the outskirts of LA, I'd also reached a point, or so I thought, of conversion. Suddenly, the traffic seemed to have quadrupled, a mosh of cars with drivers on crank, and the mess of signage amounting to a near mutiny against meaning. Watching the drivers wait for traffic to move, I might as well have been watching these broken dogs, with names like Skipper and Jeff, curled up sick in homeless peoples' shopping carts.

What am I doing here? I asked myself over and over again, like I belonged to a cult and followed a leader whom I'd never even seen. At a certain point shouldn't society wake up all at once, or person by person, until a critical mass had been achieved, and conclude that this was no way to live, and enough was enough? Doesn't the capacity to howl in protest epitomize a people shaped to shape the world according to their self and mutual interests? *I'm done with it!* Just saying it, admitting it, I felt free, recklessly free, and to keep the high going, I called Hirschman every day, sometimes even twice a day, recalling the delicious aromas in the laboratory for living he'd set up in his farm house where he'd left it all behind and started from scratch, in order to see by experimentation, what it took to be happy again. Like when we were kids, we went back and forth about the great time we had.

"There was something so peaceful…and the sound of the train! Wild how well I slept there…I haven't slept that well in years."

"Tell me about it," he said. "I hardly went a week in LA where I didn't suffer from some kind of insomnia. Sometimes my insomnia lasted forty days and forty nights, I swear, like some Jesus on speed. I'd have to go out at one-thirty to quickly down a couple of martinis at Dresden and sit and listen to jazz or whoever was covering the pack that evening and then go home and only then *hope* I'd fall asleep, but here, God be my witness," he said, "there are nights that I try to stay up and can't. There is no greater measure of the soul's health than how well one sleeps, don't you think? Nothing. It is the ultimate and truest metric, because, who was it that said—Martha Graham, maybe—*the body never lies*?"

The trip lifted me out of my nearly lethal funk. I reconnected with a few friends who asked about Hirschman, how he was *really* doing up there. I told them of the curious sights and smells and sounds, how Hirschman was canning enough food to start a small food bank.

"Yeah, but Fresno? So dull."

"You mean where your food comes from?" I said, "and all those people working and toiling to bring that food to your table?"

"Well, I didn't mean it that way."

My indignation almost surprised me, but I apparently couldn't sustain it, because within a month that sentiment had flittered away and I found myself knocking, even pounding on the door of the cult leader begging for another chance.

A group of three young women (Australians, I would presently surmise) had gathered in the long gorgeous breezeway and assembled for a picture. "Say *Chateau*," the one with the iPhone said, and all at once they said, "Chateau."

The picture taker said, "One more," and they all did it again. When they were done, they gathered around the picture taker and scrutinized what she had captured, and the picture taker said, "I'll post it." Two others from their group, that they now waved to, were just seating for lunch and ogling a youngish A-list actress that was deep in conversation over a flower petal salad, from the colorful look of it. How innocent, how ignorant these girls were of star sighting etiquette, meaning, a slow round the room look as in—did they change the umbrellas since last time?—before a matter-of-fact turning back to your own business, and, perhaps, a little-longer-study a little later on, if the star was sure to not notice, of his or her face or hair or ass or tits or legs, or of what he or she was wearing, matching the flesh and blood with the imagined ideal, how closely the simulacrum resembled the Platonic Idea. There was a life cycle to these venues, a tipping point when the star watchers far outnumber the stars, when those they come to see flee those that have come to see them. It was only a matter of time before word got out that there was no virgin to be seen at the Chateau, not even a faint burnt image on a piece of toast, and then the Chateau, like a thousand other sacred Hollywood star-sighting hot spots, will run to pot.

There were a thousand venues in this city that once needed demonic-level darkness to block out the sheer star power nightly amassed there that are now sputtering flea pits if not shuttered and gone. In fact, after a few short years in the spotlight, from the deviant rays emanating from the petitioners, all but the most leathery types, Betty White or Sly Stallone, say, suffer existential level burns. In the deepest and most tender part of their hearts, most stars actually abhor their clamoring fans; the reason they hole themselves up in private-to-the-point-of-paranoia worlds of holistic practices and vaguely shamanistic rituals. Susan from Biloxi, Sam from Little Rock, whoever from wherever, all of them come for an autograph or a high-five when they are actually coming for a golden shower or donkey punch. In fact, the greater their fame, the more base their star power grows, the more rarified grows these stars' spiritual passage, until it is inscrutable to all but themselves and those sharing, à la Oprah, their preposterous cloister. Yet there was nothing innocent, or monk or nun like about these people, no matter how deeply you plumbed their personality, or no matter how many cancer walkathons or third world charities or museum additions they sponsored, because since embryonic they were full of the most rabid, unbearable form of sociopathic narcissism, that, short of a criminal career, only an *acting* career could possibly accommodate.

I was in the middle of this thought when I looked at my watch, now worried, if Lipchitz showed up late, that I'd be forced to revise my dash-for-the meter timing. When I'd tramped up the hill toward the Chateau, I saw myself thirty years earlier, leisurely coasting down Sunset to Tower Records on my bike. *What kind of people live up there in the hills*, I wondered as a kid, and then *Maybe one day I will*, and then I was the very one living up there, and then I wasn't. What wizardry had kept them up there, and had me parking at the meter in front of the Chateau. Luck, that's what the fuck it was.

I was never *a talent* sitting in a skybox looking down upon the would-bes that had come from all over world to seek their fortune and fame, but rather I was a simple *lucky fuck* that had fallen into the right relationships with the right idea at the right time, and that for every excellent script I wrote there were tens of thousands just as excellent that simply hadn't been noticed for one stupid reason or another. But unlike many of my so-called colleagues, I had nothing to fall back on when my career came crashing down. They leaned on their wives or resurrected their family life and/or resorted to spiritual renunciation and reflection for remedy. Where once they barely knew what school their kids attended now they are all about their kids, taking them to the zoo or the Griffith Observatory or YADA classes, and then out to Langer's for, say, latkes. Where before they barely poked their yarmulkes into temple, except for the high holidays, now they were seriously considering a kosher kitchen. "Gearing up for your bat mitzvah? Aren't these the best? You have to grate the potato just so...remember how *bubbe* did them? And how's Algebra One? Soccer turning out good, scoring goals? Still friends with what's her name Sarah, Samantha?"

"Shasta, and that was in the fourth grade dad"—the kids clearly on to this oddball that has suddenly tuned in after years of tuning out, during which they'd sailed far and wide—along, naturally, with the wife—the sum of them on some seafaring carnival, with jumbo PlayStations and fusion sushi and Bikram yoga, a virtual health and pleasure boat that has now hit the great barrier reef, home to the great white shark. Even should these ex-Hollywood execs have amassed a small fortune, enough to support their lifestyles in perpetuity, even if they still enjoyed regularly quieting in the vaguely occult town of Ojai, or spoiling on the succulence of the most exotic heirloom squash, simply getting wind of news, even the most unexciting, much less *Variety* worthy, for instance, that so-and-so just got a six-week trial run for a miniseries on Oxygen—even this was enough to jumpstart a gear in their heads that in a matter of hours could grind two years worth of Kabbalah studies into mush. Now that nice two-story Tudor they bought in Calabasas, to get away from it all, suddenly seems a catastrophic decision; now that supersized tree house way up in Topanga feels like a suffocating outpost in the heart of Waziristan. Now all that devilish maturity and gray handsomeness, a la George Clooney or Ted Turner, the personification of know-how and money and networks, shows in the mirror like plain ole flesh worn thin and out, the most simple animal sagging under the pressure plate of time. Now the quick coffees with up and coming writers, where all alpha-maled up they might sermonize on where to hang out, what to do to get into the loop, who's a mensch, who'll thump on your hard-on till it goes limp, the lot of it looks like a kids theater rehearsal with adults watching dully from stiff wooden chairs wondering when it would end.

Now, I was the one watching and, apparently, rehearsing at the same time. How embarrassing, the way I skulked through the Chateau's parking garage, thinking surely one of the valets would recognize me. How embarrassing that I was both relieved and vaguely depressed when they did not. Stepping into the Chateau, its discreet and serene grandeur hushed me, in what approached a religious way, so much so that I stood for a spell in a spell watching the old fashioned elevator dial go from level 3 to level 4, before my outcast from that place came back to me with a wallop: the long leisurely afternoons and splendid nights I'd spent there with so-and-so, insouciantly splitting $300 bottles of single malt scotch, ordering whatever and occasionally pausing to admire whatever space I happened to be getting sloshed in, each its suddenly angelic yet unostentatious own, each a study in how rich people content with their lot contentedly lived as they appointed their chambers from the first to outlast a thousand plebian jags. Having signed off on bills with playboyish aplomb, I would, naturally, make my way up to one of my favorite rooms with one of any number of striking women who would warm to, and presently come to a froth in the comfy romanticism of its quarters, its quaint retro kitchens, and throwback throws, and softly creaking hard wood floor and spotless, but also lived-in and even loved-in, couches; the whole of it like being at home—not in reality, but in concept, the way we imagined it once upon a time was—while being away. Yes, the secret of the Chateau was to make it appear that nothing had changed when in fact nothing had remained the same. LA has always been like this,

I'd hear over and over again from any number of transplant idiots or self-liars, myself included. As anyone who had lived in LA long enough knew, though traffic had always been ugly it was mostly so during rush hour. Now rush hour is every hour sometimes well into the early a.m. It now took epic human resolve to drive from La Brea to Downtown, on the order of some heroic voyage demanding years in arduous training and specially tooled armor and, above all else, the kind of steely courage that in the mythical days of old was required for dragon slaying. Driving these streets we find ourselves passive and forbearing as these Hindus born into the most debased castes, or twitchy and sadistic as any tattooed hillbilly strung out on crack. Untold spiritual resources and force of will were needed to check the simple bodily longing to move forward; this violence to any common and physical sense of what travel should involve since the dawn of time when we stood on our God given two feet, required a thousand mantras to suppress, a thousand mantras to help our simple humanity cope with the paradox that such mindboggling technology as a TESLA, for instance, has effectively turned us into cows, sad cyborg cows dumbly waiting to get prodded through a bottleneck on the way to the slaughter

house, with no way around or out, not even a simple rock to sit on until the river calmed, or cave
to dip into as the windstorm passed; no this was
an artificial and relentless degradation-by-design,
one that we'd been made to suffer and passively
as ruminants. It's gotten to the point that at certain hours on certain days you might as well be
one of these boxcared Jews heading mercilessly
for Treblinka. The function of the Chateau was to
serve as a counterpoise to the abattoir, yes, it was
a small, nourishing hideaway from the dripping
and drooling pharmaceuticalized herd, an Everest
in the face of LA's evanescent spinning of culture's
made-to-evaporate curlicues, the very curlicues
the stars, holed up here, in a kind of sumptuous
bomb shelter, let's even say, relied upon for their
sustenance and survival. I chuckled, sardonical-
ly, at the cool decadence of the guests for whom,
just then, even progress seemed superfluous, as
though History had closed her books and all that
remained was to luxuriate in the weird aura left in
the human tumult's wake. You've been part of an
apocalypse, I thought, but one unfolding in such
slow motion it's been almost beautiful to watch,
a cinematic masterpiece, dazzling as a thousand
lotus flowers flowering.

I now found myself nearly sickened by the Chateau and its endlessly looping allure, a sort of hypnosis conjured for the wan pleasure of immortals; a place where there was no woe within view, and subwhites, especially so-called Latinos, forbidden, as though they tested your skin against color samples lifted from Dunn Edwards before letting you in. The human face of the Chateau, mostly twenty-something men, extraordinarily handsome and polite to the point of religious unctuousness, was actually a kind of mockery, and you almost wanted to piss right there in the lounge to see if their smooth, handsome, white baby faces, all smiles and sunshine, would flinch. They were there, of course, the subwhites, but out of sight, as all our services and food must materialize as if by fiat, because the gods brook no mish mash of wiping or scrubbing or cutting or blending or bleeding or stinking or sucking breath: it's all about the fear of friction, and how friction leads to fuckin' and fuckin' demands flesh and flesh leads to corruption and corruption leads to dissolution and dissolution leads to death. We might allow the insubstantials to materialize underground to park our cars, or buff our shoes, but only because the sub terrain in no way degrades the immaculateness of the surface; all is well so long as the lumpy tossing bowels in no way exchange fluid with the smooth nuru gelled skin.

In the deepest, darkest, and most sickening part of our veiled-to-ourselves Hollywood brains, Latinos, Indians, Pakistanis, Thais, any number of African varieties, Middle Easterners, including an occasional Sephardic Jew, whatever, it all depends on the subwhite tone of their skin, are in effect retainers, in other words, subhuman, whose function is to serve and then fade away as quietly as possible through a hundred thousand subterranean leading trap doors, down to where they can do their coarse and brown candle-lit thing for a few hours before reappearing at sunrise to start their thralldom again. Or not. Or rather, we don't actually think of them as a lot, because should one or the other subwhite disappear for good, one or the other subwhite will take his or her place, quite naturally as a machine under normal wear and tear breaks down and a replacement part is needed. No worries as subwhites do not experience pain or loss the way we do, or better they experience pain and loss but the way animals do; their internal life is not nuanced, elaborately circuited, with multiple touchy sensors and feedback loops, but rather minimal, crude, and one directional, the reason, also, they labor so effortlessly, the reason their threshold for humiliation and exploitation is infinitely higher than ours; and even should they remember the injury and thirst for revenge, no sooner than circumstances change then so do usually their outlooks and moods, as they are rigged to get along and get on with their instinctual and shared duties, like birds continue to fly in pattern, even when a hunter fells one from their flock.

The irony, evident to everyone, of course, is even as we Hollywooders expound equality and love at the top of our lungs, for the homeless and cats, dogs, and dolphins, whales, smelts, and rain forest frogs, even as we send care packages and leftover clothes home with our subwhites, even offering up our very own fatty livers for the delectation of the guilt connoisseurs, we are all the while calculating how to better live up to our carnivorous reputations. The hypocrisy is world class. Is it any wonder why every third person in this city has gastritis or GERD or irritable bowel or colitis or creeping Crone's? This city is *world class* only as a world-class GI syndrome hot spot. *Don't do this, don't do that*, they chide, while they are spending most of their waking hours, and even some of their dreamtime, doing this and precisely that. It's gotten to the point that should one disavow hypocrisy and submit one's mind to the demands of reason and common sense, or even standard arithmetic, one is immediately labeled demented, a fanatic, or an idiot. No, entertainment has become the end of culture and hypocrisy the methodology: so folded into culture it's a kind of leavening for the bread. In fact, the world seems to rise on nothing but it.

The more sinister angels of old used to begin their tales thus: "Everything we are about to say to you is a lie; now, then, listen carefully." In the land of angels we've built an earthly kingdom on this fable-spinning tradition. But there is nothing more vicious than subwhites' treatment of other subwhites. When these once-upon-a-time subterraneans make it to the surface their warm and furry blood turns oleaginous and cold, and they comport towards those they left underground with a viciousness and condescension that those born and raised aboveground could never in good conscience muster. In their heart of hearts, the candle soot that adheres to their kin's skin repulses them, and they want nothing more than to flush what microscopic residue still adheres to their own.

Behind the smiles and sunshine, winks and nods, Hollywood is full of Corleone-level hypocrisy, avarice, and malice. Yes, they have their own versions of clubs and guns and chokeholds, but their most debasing implement, I reminded myself, is simple silence: the ultimate maliciousness is simply to ignore you, to allow you to sit in a vacuum of sound until it collapses you from the inside out. As the golden hour turns into a week, and the weeks turn into muddy months, you realize that they are not going to respond, no matter what they'd been promising, if not precisely *because* they'd been promising, until you begin to feel the heft of their indifference, until, like juice being pressed out of grapes, all that is left is seeds and skins. Smiles and sunshine, it is what they hoped you'd feel, the result of their vindictive natures and the sum of their purgatorial methodology, a methodology, I might add, now mirrored across the board of our culture. By leaving you and your query hanging, they've effectively marked and owned you. Just their way of saying: *We've reached an understanding now. You are nothing. That puddle on your head is evidence. Mind you, even though I have no use for you, I still own you and can piss on you when I choose.* But, again, for all that degradation, the moment a call comes from an exec, or even an assistant to the exec, the heart suddenly turns soft and squishy and supplicant. A sickening softening of the heart, a melting away of the bitterness, and abrupt soothing of the wounds, when a miserable mother surprisingly reaches out to take her child in her arms, is very much what it feels like.

For some reason, now came to mind a couple of sound and film editors, who, once Hollywood was yanked out from beneath them, retreated into their techy dungeons and became first class conspiracy theorists, as most techies who have no other outlet for their one track techie brains typically become. They each should have turned around and gone home, but they couldn't because they had not just *left* their homes, they had spat, and shat, and pissed on their homes. Yes, just as the execs have shat and pissed on them so they have shat and pissed on those they've left behind. Most would-be actors dream of the day they might sit in the seat of fame, across from Conan or Jimmy, and wistfully express their gratitude for growing up in a small town—Tacoma or Sheboygan or Modesto—with parents and sibling and cousins and friends who BBQ'd every Sunday and never missed a ball game, and supported them every step of the way, while in their heart of hearts they'd like to stuff the entire lot of them in a gas chamber and be done with it. Every star and would-be star believes from the earliest age in his exceptionalism, and it is that very sense of exceptionalism that drives them from the boredom of home, and out of the loving or hateful or tired or indifferent arms of friends and family, into the dancing light of the lantern. But for not having acknowledged that exceptionalism, which was the star's from the start, and apparent to all but the hometown imbeciles—and even considering that Joseph and Mary needed three wise men from the east—every star and would-be star wants to turn that very lantern, in all its decrepitating might, on all those left in his or her blessed wake, exactly the way Jesus, for all his love and embrace of lepers and whores and even cynics, in the end returned with a vehemence to dish up the apocalypse.

When push came to shove, all smiles and sunshine, we were all of us forever calculating our next vertical move, what it would take and how swiftly we could make our way up, and how the person we just sat next to at the hottest new bar or coffee house, even though we just barely registered their gender, could help or hinder our ascent. It was as though there were an endless number of ladders, each out of reach of the next, and countless humans climbing up the rungs, stepping and grasping and pulling at the coattails of the person who could pull them up to the next rung, with no looking sideways, or God forbid down, except to, perhaps, all smiles and sunshine, kick in the face the person reaching for their rung. One would think that, in a city like this, those homegrown, like myself, would be different, acclimated and immunized. But so vitamin deficient is the soil, so leached of nourishment and depleted of aquifers, that even those trees grown here and established for multiple generations suffer, indeed, in many ways they are the most susceptible to disease, as they are made to contend with hundreds of thousands of avaricious foreign root stocks that are prepared to suck till the sap runs dry for the production of but a single cull, I thought, a thought which was also Hirschman's thought, as were most of these thoughts, or rather, perhaps Hirschman's thoughts had also become my thoughts, I thought.

To beat the heat, on the third day of my five day visit (yes, I *extended* it two), Hirschman decided we should take a day trip to Sequoia National Forest, about an hour and a half from town, but the route he took involved a little detour because he wanted to show me something on the way. We exited the 99, south of Kingsburg, and headed east on Avenue 384, passing peach and nectarine and plum orchards, orange groves, and vineyards, all sagging, if not quavering from the exertion, it seemed, of holding up all that summer fruit.

"Amazing place," he said, "which should go without saying. I mean, there are only maybe a dozen places in the world where food can grow like this. Sure, high class weeds and sundry little squatty and gnarled things grow all over the world, but only a few places can grow nearly everything, all the choicest fruits and nuts—plums and pluots and almonds and pistachios and pomegranates and persimmons and pears and more—all of it in all their ripe splendor; because to grow them in all their ripe splendor requires an ultra rare convergence of elements, as improbable as the convergence of our founding fathers, in one place in time."

He described how the valley was once a great inland sea that had evaporated, leaving it chock full of minerals, including calcium from the shells and bones of sea life, and that over millions of years the Sierras deposited on top of all this their rich erosion. The water tables beneath the land and the mountains with their vast snowpack, and what they call a Mediterranean climate. "Winters cold enough to put the trees to sleep without killing them, mild springs, and summers with especially intense light and the driest, you can feel it, heat." And then there were the great dams we built, and the canals that fed the farms, and, of course, the farmers and the laborers, "a majority illegal, let's just say it for what it is, and their beyond-human stamina," that shed these trees of millions of tons of fruit in a period of just a couple of months alone.

Now we passed an intersection and slowed on a place called Yettem, population 211, so a little sign claimed. A concrete canal ran parallel a road and here and there small foot bridges led across it to "town": a dozen or so of what appeared to be squatters shacks thrown up between chicken pens and broken down cars and rusting farm equipment, around which a few shirtless little boys, and even a couple of shirtless little girls—what with the heat, I suppose, who was to judge—were playing with hoses. In defiance, it almost seemed, of all that squalor, and maybe half a mile up the road, I could see a beautiful red brick church with a bell tower up front, and just behind it a white dome, all of it rising three stories or more against the Sierra Nevada.

"What an unlikely place for such a sweet church; this place is further out than nowhere."

"It's an Armenian church," Hirschman said, and explained how they'd come here even before the genocide to establish a community, and that such was their faith and feeling for this place—the land, the air, the water, and the mountains—that they called it Yettem.

"In Armenian it means Eden, which maybe explains the naked kids back there. Anyway, that's what they thought they'd stumbled upon, and maybe even returned to, because the Central Valley most likely reminded them of the mythic Ararat Valley, the so-called cradle of civilization, where Noah got things going again, and also where the Armenians were driven from."

The image of those Armenians volleyed me straight back into that car with my mother, that strange exchange, and small mocking spit of dirt from her mouth. From not wanting to hurt Hirschman's feelings, and maybe, too, from embarrassment, until that moment, I'd kept it to myself.

He listened to me now recount the episode, and said, "Almost inconceivable, I mean, this contempt for where our food comes from. For most of human history, extending back fifty thousand years, people brought sacrifices, even human sacrifices to their land of milk and honey; sung hymns to its glory and told of its gargantuan power in their lore and worried obsessively over droughts, floods, pests, and diseases that might visit these lands. Not to say that we're the only advanced culture that saw their farmers as dolts, but no culture has proven so ignorant, and even contemptuous of where their foods come from, to the point that any day of the week you can find people throwing their noses up at the Great Central Valley while munching on a peach grown here. It's one thing to take for granted where your food comes from, but this contempt is quite unique, and points to the unique decadency of this culture. The way I see it, both north and south of this great state, picture here a vast machine of agriculture, that for them is not the smell of life teeming, but the smell of death churning; yes, their true fear is the vast, monotonous machinery of agriculture that feeds the vast monotony of humanity, all stampeding towards dissolution and death.

"They fear the billions of pounds of pale tomatoes dropping from the heavens onto their overripe heirloom pumpkin heads, and yes, let's admit it and quit any romanticism here, these farmers have shrunken to midget size the vast plethora—the thousands of windows onto the world, that millennia of vast rainbows of fruit and vegetable varieties that once sprung to life across this planet—to a stupid few, but this is only because of Americans' sheer revulsion to anything that is different today from what it was yesterday, that is different from one year to the next, anything that has a dent or scar or bruise, in sum, any mark of nature on it; and yes, these farmers have produced the most tasteless tomatoes ever farmed on the face of the earth, virtually cryogenic clones engineered to taste near to nothing when they arrive, and yet, at the same time, fit for a museum. But this is precisely because this is what tasteless and optics-driven America expects: food plentiful and good-looking and especially cheap, so that they can better squander their hard-earned dollar on another super-sized optics machine. Sure, the most outlandish invention in the world is the modern supermarket, nothing more insulting, even bludgeoning, to the human soul, but—at least when one walks into one—one should have a sense of reverence for the people and places those foods have come from. The waxing and waning of the seasons, the thinning and growing of light, the blooming storms and baffling fog. The sun that blasts down on the slow ripening fruit and sky, and ultimately, the putrefaction of everything— even our very sun—all of this is a reminder of the cycle of life, its winter storms and pacific fall afternoons—that we can in no way tolerate in the empire of eternal sunshine, because all of it ultimately echoes our own dissolution and death. If you walk and work the very ground that becomes a part of your body, you can't help but have this intimate connection to it, even if that intimacy also marks your corruptibility; and because we have no idea where our food comes from, we essentially have no idea where we are living, and hence we might as well be living anywhere, or nowhere. We might as well be anything, or nothing, or rather a heartless, hearthless, free-floating mutt culture, that lifts its leg, pisses, and trots off. But as the Class A soil is depleted, and wells run dry and global warming sets its teeth, and these places, let's even call them palaces, where food like this can grow, become scarcer and scarcer, that arrogance and ignorance and fear will get its comeuppance. Mark my word: oil will look like nothing next to fruits and vegetables and maybe even grains, and especially the water that feeds it all, in the future."

We were now at the entrance to the park, at least the part of it called the Sequoia National Monument. My memory of the Sierras had faded since last I visited it as a kid. I had the token mental picture-postcard of trees spectacular in scale, but now I found it was less what my eye took in than what the rest of my senses did as we hiked; the alternating sun and shade, the crunch of needles, the buoyancy of the air and the strangely sweet and fine dust that rose from beneath our shoes, and most of all, the sheer physicality of the trees next to my miniscule own. All of it hushed me, as it must've Hirschman, because for the hour or so we made our way down trail, neither of us, who were ever at a loss for words, said a word, until we reached General Sherman, ramifying before our eyes like a giant muddy geyser, frozen in state, a natural tour de force far beyond human reckoning.

We stood there studying it. "What makes it great isn't just its size," Hirschman said, "but that it's kept going, inch by perilous inch, against such impossible odds, for a millennium or more, alongside its brethren. Don't you think? Now that once little sapling is one of the largest living things on the face of the earth, and the original name, not Sherman but Karl Marx." If it weren't coming from him I surely would've considered a yarn the tale he now told of how a group of socialists had come upon it in the late nineteenth century, and seeing its stature and might named it after the man whose work they believed would shake the foundation of earth on which it stood. "Naturally, that didn't sit well with the powers that be."

We moved on, and after three hours hiking we took a break in the shade where I thanked him, for the time, for putting me up, for putting up with me. "I needed this like it was nobody's business. I needed to get away. Away from LA, and away from myself."

I reached out to grab a plum from my small backpack, and he said, "Your hands have stopped shaking."

"Were they shaking?" I asked, taking a good look at them.

"Your whole being was shaking; it's just that there's no hiding your hands."

"Yep, you're right on the money, as usual. I've been in a bad way." It was then that I laid it all out, every humiliating detail, most of which I'd kept secret, even from him. How I dropped Facebook and Twitter, and especially LinkedIn, whose vast arterial structure I followed down to the stupidest, spindliest, capillaries, feeding the most redundant tissue cells; how it got to the point that I was dragging my feet in little choppy steps like a strung out crack addict; how I wanted whatever dark power was hovering over me to snuff me out, a mere thing among things; but it did not snuff me out, no, it flapped its dark merciless wings in front of my face, mocking me for how little power I had left in my person to draw it closer and put the whole human affair to rest. I would not commit suicide. I was too much a coward for that. I hadn't, or probably *couldn't* reach that point where my tolerance for pain was exhausted and death became inevitable, and perhaps even delicious. I suppose as a Jew, my threshold for pain was infinitely greater than my will to death. It was like inside of me was some sociopathic bully, some SS wannabe that kept the rest of me around just so that he could keep his human toying going.

"It's a good thing, you didn't listen to that bully, that screaming homunculus inside of you, inside of each of us," he said. "He's run ripshod over nearly everyone these days, the little distorted man screaming to be taken seriously. Worse, no one any longer knows how to quiet him down. First there was the land, the place, then this, nature, in the concrete and abstract," he said looking around us, "in all its awe inspiring magnificence; and side by side with this there was God, and finally art, but now in the absence of those the world is at its screaming mercy. In fact, the way I see it, all of culture's current efforts have been engineered to amplify the scream to the boiling point."

That's when he turned to me and suggested I move to Fresno, to, why not, one of those places off the mall. To try and fashion a hearth there. "Maybe you'll be able to quiet that little man down here, like I did."

I came up from these thoughts to find the patio tables now all but full, only a handful reserved seating empty, and impossibly, and through their appetizers even, the Australians, notwithstanding all their native Australian sociability, holding steadfast to their smartphones, a near public rebuke, at this juncture, of the superfluity of the souls gathered there with them, as though they were juggling nothing short of dispatches from or to extraterrestrials on the next steps required to subjugate the mortals down below. *How many times,* I wondered, *had I been similarly seated, in apparent equanimity, posting here and texting there, only to be on the inside of a monstrous whirligig screaming for attention, surrounded by monstrous whirligigs likewise screaming for attention.*

"Never in the history of humanity," Hirschman said, "has there been such a mad rush to reach nowhere; and a virtual nowhere at that, with Hollywood leading the charge." These e-mails and texts, Twitter and Insta-this and Insta-that…even when the ringer was turned off, the phone's buzz somehow still surviving, like the retching of some small sick animal. The way people came up from the tweeting all abstracted, trying to mentally shore up for the world of modest human commerce, oblivious to whatever magic or monotony the moment might humbly offer; as though life were a chimera up until it had been posted, whereupon it became reality and was subsumed in the oceanic accounting of human history and needn't be troubled over any longer.

Today the Australians are recording for friends and family and themselves, for posterity, but if they were to stay in LA, within half a year, all their native Australian conviviality would leach away, and out of that void would arise a banshee like cry. Even more, they would soon discover that for every half a million hollerers there were only a handful of ears up to the challenge of taking that hollering in; hence, the tens of thousand of hired ears, psychologists and psychiatrists and life coaches and therapists, counselors—marriage and family and personal (let alone the lower-tiered ears of hairdressers and massage therapists and nail stylists)—all at the ready, all of whom might have concluded after a few sessions (had their livelihoods not depended upon it), that there was nothing behind the words worth discovering. No path of words leading to a clearing, nor a wall of words worth taking down to expose what-the-fuck-made-this-person-up, but rather, that words, and words alone, were all that this very storming disaster sitting across from them was made of, and that should the chatter halt, the whole of it would disintegrate like a dust devil into thin air. In fact, entire conversations in LA consist of nothing more than two or three or more homunculi sitting at a table and waiting their turn to scream at the top of their lungs over whatever the newest cocktail is. You could almost see the bawling toddler rising from his diarrhea diapered seat to tell of why so-and-so at a certain casting agency really, truly, felt they were right for this or that part, but that this or that or the other thing kept it from happening.

It's no wonder people stayed on the surface here. The simplest existential question can set in motion an excruciating and endless exegesis that would test the likes of a Mother Theresa; nobody disturbs the surface in fear of generating a tsunami from the neurotic and tectonic deep of the babbler's brain. If only now and then people told simple stories rather than yakked inexhaustibly on about their every trivial setback. How refreshing it would be, once in a blue moon, to hear a simple story where the protagonist wasn't the blathering storyteller's twitchy little ego. How refreshing it would be to hear a simple yarn that began with something like, "I had this Uncle Pete who had an alligator for a best friend," or "this crazy cousin of mine once pissed off a balcony straight on the head of a cop, I swear…"—a simple tale of mischief, triumph, or even ignominy, that children, but also the child in each of us, is game to hear. Maybe it's because people here are loath to tell such stories in fear of revealing their maggot like past, or maybe they picture their maggot like past an irrelevancy as in short order they'll be commuting on an astral dimension that neither history nor memory might reach. Instead, what they do is endlessly dismember and dissect the moment, turning over the most miniscule detail of their latest career success or, mostly, fiasco, until everyone wants to flee. If people cannot talk about their restless selves and what abscesses and boils currently plague them, they have nothing to really talk about—just as people with actual abscesses and boils can hardly do anything but worry and itch over these abscesses and boils. So the emotional/psychological abscesses and boils that plague Hollywood types keep them from being able to speak of anything else. Everyone is waiting to get their turn to tell of their latest success or fiasco that smells like perfume to their teller and like death to the listener. Even news of the most petty and ultimately immaterial audition or gig is belched out as though it were the highest order French perfume. Everyone is waiting to flee from the stench only to turn around and produce their own stench, from which others will naturally flee. Everyone then is reeling away from the stench of everyone else, except for those few intimates and friends who have gotten used to the stench, like serfs who've known nothing but an outhouse are used to the outhouse's stench. Even if you come to Los Angeles without this stench, within a year it will be oozing from your pores.

This city neuroticizes if not necrotizes you as efficiently as any Congolese child-warrior boot camp, I thought. To simply orient one's animal brain to the ego hullaballoo one daily awakens to, a good three-quarter of the city pop, on balance, three or four pills. ADD and ADHD are as common here as headaches and sniffles in most other cities. In a pinch, from the typical Hollywood type's medicine cabinet—I submit my own as a case study—you could open a small apothecary of homeopathic and conventional meds. There was hardly a person here, even priests and professors, that weren't suffering from one or another neurosis bordering on functional psychosis. Yes, at the bottom of all human beings is a retarded homunculus screaming to be heard; Hirschman was right, but most people from the earliest possible age place a gag on it, and those who refused to gag themselves, or be gagged, migrate to LA, so that the entirety of the city boils over with screaming homunculi, making the usual human exchange all but impossible without mortifying yourself from head toe with thrashing homunculi spit.

My mother was a screaming homunculus with the muzzle off; my father was a screaming homunculus with the muzzle on; and I achieved the dubious distinction of being both at once! Just then, the bitterness I felt toward my mother and her preposterous will came back to me with vengeance, the way she handed her meager estate away to ideas, abstractions, the opera, museums, and other ridiculous cultural venues, spreading the love in equal measure to eight in all, or rather nine, how ironic, as my slice of the pie was the same as theirs.

Hirschman, as usual, had it right: Nobody but dolts (like my mother) believe in art anymore, especially artists, he said, "who have been forced to concede that culture finds their work ridiculous and, even where brilliant, utterly superfluous, as society is now inundated with fictions, as a matter of fact, nothing but; and the commonplace has become as much a work of art, if not more so, than anything so-called artists create. The arts are long dead, only the artists refuse to go to the funeral, or maybe it's more accurate to say they've been too busy fucking the corpse, and wondering, too, I suppose, why it won't come. Even so, art should relentlessly pursue a return, yes, a near resurrection, to restore to itself its sacred mission of making one feel at home in the world, if not literally, making a home in the world, even if the whole idea of home has been obliterated, and culture has relegated art's function to decoration, however dazzlingly fabulous, darling."

Sitting at the Chateau, waiting for Lipchitz, I thought, perhaps if I'd let my mom know how bad things had gotten she would've shown some pity on her only child, but, honestly, all I could think of was how, even collapsed by the lung cancer, she would've managed to howl in laughter at my own collapse. There was nothing the woman loathed more than fear and psychological feebleness in men: and there was no greater sign of these than a man holed up in a room the way I was for months, sabotaging by default life itself, tuned out to the hustle and bustle of culture and commerce that the great and rare American cities like New York and Chicago and Los Angeles offered.

A family of four, who now took a table next to mine, calmed these thoughts down some. The kids looked straight out of Bergman's *Fanny and Alexander*, all dressed in cute outfits, the boy with a blue button down, bow tie, and white shorts, and the girl in a delicate pink dress. I began thinking that maybe they were from Europe— Switzerland, or possibly France. They were politely looking about the room like kids should look about such a beautiful room but which those of that class rarely do, as they've seen everything there is to see and it all ends up looking the same. The mother, too, she was as lovely a woman as they come, without having to nip and tuck it into existence, and I wondered now what kept me from finding such simple loveliness and having such a family rather than turning every relationship into a battle among whining migraines, and, in the end, having no children to show for it, thank god I guess. She was explaining the menu, with the kids on either side of her nodding at whatever it was she was suggesting, and then she put the menu down and put her hands together like when someone wants to think deeply, or pray.

I might've had a normal family life had I settled down in a city where raising your kids wasn't so debasing; just watching my friends shuttling and carpooling and dumping and picking up their kids, this way and that, through butchering traffic jams, from one place to another, for soccer, then softball, then acting class and ballet. Mapping it was like mapping the zigzagging flight pattern of a wasp bent-on-revenge, a fearsome complexity that even the most advanced mathematical models would collapse trying to capture.

If you aren't knocking down a quarter million, at least, just getting your kids decently educated in LAUSD proved a full-time and fanatical affair. By force of duty the poor parents are dropped into what can only be described as a *theater of war*, with hardly a compass or map, much less a rifle or grenade, to battle their way in. There was no question of letting one's kids "tough it out" beyond K-5 in their local school, because what with guns and crank, schoolyard scuffles ain't what they used to be—a full third of the student body dropouts anyhow, cuz-whaz-da-point in knowledge, truth, and even beauty, when bling and boom and booty is all ye know and all y'all need to know.

Neighborhood kids, sometimes even siblings, are scattered far and wide to private and magnet and charters, forcing parents to play connect the dots at a humongous and deranged scale just to draw a normal social life outside of school for their otherwise isolated like lunar lander kids. *You want to see Sarah this month—again?! Oy vey!*

Starting from kindergarten, the pressure on these exhausted Hollywood parents, one and all, was immense, because Stacey might fall behind Tanner across the street, both that have definitely fallen behind Blythe up the block, all of whom will never reach the stellar heights of that Korean boy, just moved in, whose genius was the obvious, straight As, 150 IQ kind, whereas the genius of most Hollywood kids is less obvious, if not positively ethereal, to the extent that the combined diagnostic powers of Freud, Jung, Rogers, even Stanford and Binet, would be taxed to fathom it. In fact, I think it's fair to say that in most cases the more retarded their kid, by all quantitative measures, the more the parents believe the child possesses some qualitative genius, even if, heretofore, and well into the future, it remains a mystery to all but the occult sciences.

For Hollywood kids, every trip or fall is padded a thousand times over with a thousand squishy pillows, rendering them spineless, thin skinned, without any internal defenses, and only a kind of prissy bluster to muster; in sum, utterly unable to negotiate the seething world just outside their zip codes. Let's face it: the innocence and wonderful obliviousness of childhood, all the rich inner discovery world of children, is all but gutted in a place like this, and instead they are made to take it all in like tourists on those preposterous double decker buses with their neurotic laryngitic parents as the guides.

This is why I wrote this script, for these kids, for the kid that I was, and the kid that I still am, the one that continues to scream at the hypocrisy, the kid in me, in all of us, that refuses to shut up; and it will either restart or utterly terminate my career. In any case, it will be my last will and testament, so to speak, and, yes, I would relish announcing a deal to my friends, but that announcement, thinking, once again, of Hirschman, would be more revenge than anything else, I now admitted to myself; the thrust of such an announcement would most definitely be a desire to crush them, especially those that stood by as my life and all that I had lived for spiraled into poverty. Yes, the deliciousness of revenge I'd know as my so-called associates, former agents, and managers watched me take off again would be in its deepest and darkest essence the deliciousness of the last meal before the electric chair. That *yes* would, in fact, be less a *yes* to myself as a *no* to them, and a *no* to them would, in the end, prove a *no* to myself.

Just then, a text from Lipchitz popped up: "rnng lte; lks 1:15 ish." *Ish*. *Ish* could mean just about anything-ish. What the fuck with *lte*? We're talking one letter here. As though he were sending a cross-ocean dispatch that required a middleman and machine like telegraphing offices of old. And why didn't he have one of those auto fill-in functions anyway? Maybe Lipchitz had fallen into indigence, as well; maybe he was still using a BlackBerry. Even though word around town was that two of Lipchitz's recent projects had been green-lighted, maybe your desperate person shouldn't have so casually dismissed IMDB that had him shooting blanks for the last four years.

For how fast decisions were made and fortunes reversed, a week in showbiz was the equal of a full life cycle in any other biz. No matter how high up the mountain the project had climbed, or the number of corpses and oxygen canisters it had passed on its way to glory, there was always a chance, if not an excellent probability, that it would run out of breath and be left to rot, and from just behind it a cockeyed and spastic replacement would materialize and make it to the summit. Precisely like God could have chosen an infinite number of worlds, but chose to bring into existence this ridiculous and cockeyed and spastic one, so more often than not, it seemed, the most ridiculous and cockeyed and spastic project would get chosen and brought to creation.

Almost to make my point, "No worries," I texted back. "Little late myself. See you then at one." As soon as I hit **send,** I thought, *Who writes "you" when there's "u," and who the hell writes "one" when "1" will obviously do?*

From the corner of my eye, I caught a flash of yellow; Skinny Jeans, obviously recovered from the pistol whipping, was walking in lazy figure 8s in the breezeway, quietly cackling and nodding optimistically into his cell phone, demonstrating the mindboggling tensile strength, if not indestructability, the job required. However much I tried, I never had that level of blinkered optimism; in fact, at best, I fought pessimism off only in fits and starts. Only when writing did my heart unfold and my mind grow wide and generous; only when I opened myself up to the world, in the way that serious writing requires you to open to the world, did I leave my cynicism behind and tunnel through to something resembling light, to beauty and hope, and even a small taste of grace.

Hirschman was right: there was hardly anyone, even great novelists—Faulkner and Fante, Fitzgerald and Steinbeck, Saroyan and even Nathaniel West—none of them were able to resist the seductions of this whore-place; seductions which I was and, apparently, still am susceptible to, even after having placed a deposit on my apartment, even after having committed myself, so I thought, body and soul, to Fresno.

Maybe his delay was a blessing in disguise. I planned on eating and, for that matter, picking up the check to mask my privation, and now that he was going to be late there was a good chance that he would have already lunched, saving me the cash equivalent of a tank of gas, more or less the amount, I suspected, my sclerotic Mercedes would ingest before it gave up the ghost—even after I tried three code blue–level rescues, even after dumping a good five thousand dollars into the shithole of an Armenian, then Korean, and, finally, a Craigslist sourced Salvadoran mechanic in Downey whose "garage" was, behold, his garage! That long-winded text was a dead give away of your nearly middle-aged mind set; indefensible when the snarky, casually sadistic exuberance of punks idling around a skateboard park is the industry's emotional gold standard. You need to

choose your battles more carefully! Bringing a
nuclear solution where an Uzi or two will do is
what has gotten you into trouble from the start.
Besides, there is nothing in the least wrong with
this kind of abbreviated communication; it is simple shorthand, what your average secretary way
back when used when taking dictation.

Lipchitz had probably already reserved a table for us, in which case I would just take that
table and order an appetizer and wait until he
showed to order something sizeable. I hadn't had
but a cup of Peet's coffee and half a Sam's sesa-
me bagel down on Larchmont and, quite predict-
ably, the martinis had pirated my system. I waved
down the waitress and mentioned I'd be moving
to lunch and asked if she would please transfer the
bill to the table.

At the receptionist's little desk, the beautiful,
buxom, brown-haired receptionist asked, "Under
what name should I find your reservation?"

"Lipchitz."

"I don't recall seeing his name," she said, obviously recognizing the name.

Maybe he gave another name, and then I start
thinking maybe it was under his corporate name,
and then I thought, *What the fuck is his corporate
name?*—since these people start and fold up cor-

porations as casually as caterers do tables. Not likely that he put it under my name, but on the small chance I gave that to her anyway.

She shook her head definitely *no,* and then said, "I'm sorry." The way she said it, stretching the *I'm* out to the point of pity, made me wince, and in retaliation I began to scrutinize the off-shape of her mouth, the way the left side drooped, almost imperceptibly, like maybe she'd just come in from some dental work, the only thing actually worthy of censure as the rest of her was heart-woundingly beautiful.

"Do you have seating for two?" I asked, at this point kind of panicking, and she asked me to "please wait," then she walked off to another station efficiently, yet elegantly, and stopped to query a handsome forty-ish gentleman in a gorgeous, what looked Boss, suit, and that man bobbled his head as in *maybe.*

She came back and said she could seat me in the dining room—that, of course, is where those who could not be seated on the gorgeous and coveted patio were seated—and added, "But at two forty-five we will have a reserved party arriving. Will that work with your schedule?"

That would give us a good hour and a half, but if Lipchitz showed up later than he claimed, say, more like 1:45, we'd be forced to leave the table, I predicted, just as we were entering the merciless negotiation stage. But, at this juncture, once again, likely because the martinis had wildly opened my appetite, I said, "I think that will work. We'll just move to the bar if we aren't finished with our meeting by then."

"Follow me."

"I hope this suits you just fine," she said, and indeed, it was a lovely table in the dining room, as if there were an ugly one. "Enjoy your lunch; and if you don't mind me saying, I really admire your writing. We studied *Fire of Proof* at NYU."

"Thank you. It's one of my favorite scripts, and they did a terrific job with it," I said, almost sheepishly.

As I watched her attractiveness now retreat— who gives a shit about her almost imperceptible drooping lip, that, if the result of a fatally dead nerve from infection or whatnot, poor thing, had probably doomed her career and landed her as a receptionist at the Chateau, not just tempo- rarily until she hit it big, but permanently until the vast balance of her excellent looks petered out—I confess, I just about cried, as in when you get the birthday present you most desperately wanted but assumed your parents couldn't afford.

She seemed so sincere now, and almost artful in her conscientious gait, definitely a kind of quiet, sweet natured stunner, probably a Connecticut or New Hampshire girl that naturally chose the east rather than west coast for dramatic training after some boarding school upbringing, Hotchkiss or the like. I looked for a ring on her wedding finger and didn't see one, and began thinking of asking her out, but then immediately I evacuated the thought, because whatever chance there was for whatever to develop between us would be dead on arrival the moment I walked her to my car: scratched and dented, and with hubcaps scuffed to the point of furriness, it broadcast wretchedness in a way that only over-the-hill luxury cars can; yet I hung onto it like some starlet who hangs on to twenty-year-old headshots that look *maaaybe* like her daughter?

The waiter came by, handed me a menu, and asked if I'd care for something to drink, and since I was sitting there and in such a good mood from the flattery, in spite of my dashed hopes of dating the flatterer, I ordered my third martini. For some reason, I now wondered doubtingly about Hirschman's statement that scriptwriting required an essentially childish, black-and-white, single-minded state of mind, because, as with a child, he claimed, the movie must develop along certain set points, with little accent color accents thrown in. Hirschman was a genius, if not a shaman, for sure, but even he was capable of some outrageous opinions and criticisms; and it now also dawned on me that with his pointless death on that country road, I'd built a kind of mote around his memory, and was protecting it, and indeed his every idea, as if to challenge but one or two of them would amount to abandoning the castle. How about his strange assertion that once you took on the vantage point of a novelist you were doomed as a screenwriter, if not doomed as a human being, because, above and beyond anything else, the human mind is structured to see reality from its point of view, and only from its point of view, and will stop at nothing to win others' over to its point of view, even to the point of death; while a novelist, worth their salt, will stop at nothing to account for every conceivable and inconceivable point of view.

In a novel, you work your way not to the truth but to the manifold of reality... Novelists' brains are often taken over by a great wind that flings all the windows onto reality open at once; this full-spectrum-split-second awareness of the manifold that transcends the peephole vision of the common brain is often beyond the skills of the writer to manage. He goes about trying to capture all that he sees and is left laid out near-dead for the effort; and thus, the most serious element in the "craft" of writing has to do with developing the tools to deal with this manifold, and until those tools are developed most novelists are blind-sided stupid.

The difference between a serious novelist and a screenwriter is that a serious novelist must contend not only with a thousand choices, what any writer of any genre must contend with, but a thousand points of view, each taking in the moment in its totality from that perspective. One's perspective is not part of a whole, but the whole in itself; further, there are not competing wholes but rather each whole reflects reality perfectly, and such is the nature of reality that it can accommodate them all without contradiction. Reality is too much to bear, not because it casts doubt on what you previously believed to be true, but because it includes what you previously held to be true and a universe more. The problem has never been there is no meaning, but that there is too much of it. Reality is not a matter of addition, $1 + 1 + 1$, nor is it a matter of negation, $(1 -1) + (1-1)$, but rather of multiplication, $1 \times 1 \times 1$, into infinity; a world, in other words, beyond stay or negation; a world, in other words, of pure *affirmation. Los Angeles* (per Hirschman's last novel set during the 1992 Los Angeles Riots) *had the chance to become the living, breathing manifestation of this reality, and all it managed to do was turn into a tribal war zone*—(Hirschman).

People like Hirschman can either lift you up to a different dimension, or utterly destroy you; or rather, they utterly destroy you even as they lift you up. I shook my head to clear it, of Hirschman, and then, unable to do so, balked at Hirschman's hypothesis: wasn't this motley mix of peoples and tongues, however tribal, also the saving grace of this place? Wasn't the fact that Los Angeles was one of the most ethnically diverse cities in America something we embraced?

In fact, the only authentic people left in LA are the tribal ones, I thought, those that have come here from somewhere else, or fitted their own authentic society within our farcical one: long time LA Blacks, and Latinos, Thai and Armenians, and Ethiopians, and a hundred different others. They are the only people saving this city from utter ruin, even though, to be honest and not sugarcoat the thing, it's nearly impossible to penetrate their ghetto reality outside of an occasional nibble at their food. The Chinese in their Monterrey Park underworld of call girls and strange slaughtered meats; or the Armenians in Glendale or the Thais in Thaitown or the Koreans in Koreatown who, let's face it, have managed to mimic, to the point of parody, all the posturing of Hollywood and, at the same time, shut themselves off from Hollywood like some paranoid village idiot standing guard at the ancestral shithole. Walk into one of their supermarkets or appliance stores, or even a shabby auto shop and they will virtually shoo you away, as though you were a stray that had slipped in through the back door. Bent over their mung bean pancakes and gochujang stews, they have effectively given the middle finger to LA; their comeuppance, I suppose, from 1992, when we picked our noses as their neighborhoods were fire stormed to clinkers. In fact, every ethnic person who spends any time in this city eventually turns into a ridiculous anime version of his former self. Within half a year of landing here, the French, or Argentinians, Italians or Russians or Afghanis, are leached of their native goodness and only their flamboyant corpse, like these empty and ostentatious Easter Eggs, survives.

Though I love the old Jews settled here before and after our calamity—those that opened liquor stores and delis, and went to temple now and then, those that fought piecemeal for every

square inch of the world they have today—their
kids, and their kids' kids, are nothing more than
relentless whining neurotics, a dripping draining
sponge of need that even *sickening self-absorption*
falls short describing. Even the stupidest Jew, let's
face it, has better than average intelligence, yet
for all that brainpower I've never seen a people so
congenitally obnoxious and emotionally obtuse.
But they are nothing next to the Orthodox; the
head-scarved moms in their minivans bursting
with kids charging to their next appointment like
chemo patients on high dose steroids; the men,
during the high holidays, chanting their dreadful
tribal songs at the top of their bottomless lungs.
On Saturday mornings, the endless measure of
them scuttling back and forth from their crannies
like roaches, their black and sticky selves afraid
of making contact with any species not of their
own; the kids trailing like characters in a night-
mare, where what you put on at the costume party for a laugh you are forced to wear for the rest
of your life. Not that you could blame them, or
any of these ethnic people for folding inward to
the point of farce, as only ethnic people, with one
foot in this country and one foot out, can see that
putting one's faith, much less one's children, at the
mercy of this city—this animated, indeed, acro-

batic cadaver—has become unthinkable. Whereas from the beginning of time the culture helped raise the child, here the culture razes the child; yes, we've gone from raising to razing, from nurturing to denaturing, from developing to denuding, from aiding to abetting the most degenerate attitudes and and behaviors, I thought, waiting for Lipchitz who, at this juncture, might've decided instead for a Dirty Sanchez at some West Hollywood sex dungeon.

Again, whereas from the beginning of civilization the child was left to society for the roughhew, with the parents applying the finishing touches, here the parents must do both the roughhew and finishing, all the while inoculating their children as best they can from the non-stop poisons the culture is releasing into the city's bloodstream. If it weren't for the African Americans, and especially the Latinos, recent immigrants and even the so-called undocumented, this city would have died from toxic overload long ago. Without these people's antidote—their honest labor and faith in kinship and daily dose of generosity— LA would have turned into a cosmic singularity long ago, a remorseless corpse whose potent gravity not even light can escape. Still, let's admit it, what world-class derelicts second and third generation Latinos have become, receding backwards at break-neck speeds to better demolish all their parents built up for them. Rather than honoring the sacrifice their parents made, they spit and shit on that sacrifice; rather than continue up the ladder, the girls drop off the ladder to get knocked up, and the men drop off the ladder to knock each other off—chilling only to cover every inch of their flesh with one and another image or script, as though they weren't human so much as abandoned fields taken over by weeds.

Still, one is tempted to say; enough is enough of any of these Latinos, documented, undocumented, or here for a hundred years. Like an endless dust storm covering everything in its path, this brown and monotonous redundancy keeps coming and coming, pitiless in ferocity. The gringos' assumption that they will forever be little squirrels running around the park and foraging for nuts is nothing more than a psychological defense against their demographic reality, pushing the city to a disastrous tipping point. If Latinos should ever become unified, they will, in a matter of a decade, turn LA into a mirror image of their stifled and stupid inertia-filled homeland.

Then there are the Armenians, with their mechanically challenged Mercedes and gross gold crosses planted in their burly steel wool chests; and how about those eyes set like thousand year old mud pies? The rats raced from the bowels of their cumin stinking ships, flooded the city, and quick as that set up a thousand graft and corruption and exploitation shops. Rather than planting roots in the land that took them in, their first thought was how to best desiccate the hard-earned top soil, just like they desiccated the top soil of the USSR until even the lowliest tuber stood no chance.

Even the Thais, with their sticky rice and sticky massage parlor beds, disgusting. There is no mosaic in this city. The very notion is a farce. There is only a wedding dish smashed on the asphalt, a shambolic disaster. We are at each other's throats, no matter what they say, no matter how pastel we-are-the-world they air brush these sub-cultures, especially the black or African Americans, or whatever they call themselves these days, who on the broken bones of their parents and ancestors, and in but a single generation, have degenerated to what can only be described as a slovenly matriarchy. The men either in prison, or roaming the streets in packs, like wolves on the lam. Cynicism and degradation, hissing and dissing and pissing on their girls, whose sole escape is getting impregnated by any random *baby-daddy* and spending the balance of their lives in front of the TV hearth, smoking crack, talking smack, and collecting welfare. In seconds any dimwit could conclude the cultural abyss these people have lowered themselves into, but educated people spend years trying to unfigure it out. Indeed, a vast majority of the so-called intellectuals in this city are now vested head to hoof in how to unfigure out what any honest half-wit could figure out. Let's even call it a kind of Cottage Industry, I thought, and picked up the menu: *Chick Pea Panissee with Kale, Quinoa, Walnuts and Beets; Herb Crusted Arctic Char with Asparagus; Bronzino with Belugia Lentils and Salsa Verde,* etc. Even though I had no idea what half of it meant, all of it, down to the *Potted Smoke Trout,* set my appetite ablaze, while at the same time waterboarding it, because, *across the board,* even to the cup of ginger iced tea, the prices hovered near derision: "You came here to the Chateau thinking you could afford it! Lowlife. Try Norms down the street."

I knew it would be an expensive lunch, but I honestly had no idea the prices had grown to approach criminal accountability. It hit hard on the lovely buzz I had going. You are paying for the servers and lighting and air conditioning, the

grounds keepers and car parkers, I reminded myself, all the subterraneans; you are paying for almost everything but the food, so relax. I'd almost
forget about parking. Lipchitz's delay would give
me an opportunity to meter up and maybe even
avoid having to excuse myself during our meeting.

I left my wallet and phone on the table and
quickly made my way out of the Chateau, through
the garage, and into the lavish sunlight. As I
rummaged for quarters in the revolting middle
compartment of my revolting car, I thought, what
does it matter what the beautiful receptionist
thought of my earlier work? The city is full of
thousands of writers with an excellent portfolio of
films living just like I am living, in near squalor in
a near dungeon.

From the martinis, I presume, I was strangely
sweating by the time I got back to my table, where
I noticed a couple was seated to my right, locals,
it looked like, for a late lunch: the man, middle-aged and super handsome, with a full head
of salt-and-pepper stylishly wind tousled hair,
wore an Armani sweat suit; the women, in Juicy
Couture, was considerably younger, or maybe
not, because upon closer inspection the full lips
and cheeks and smooth forehead were quarrelling
with the turkey runnels in her neck. At any Hol-

lywood party you could happen upon the enigma of women in their mid-fifties flipping their hair about and chatting with the edgy vivaciousness of teens at a bat mitzvah, just like this one was now doing with her male companion. Past thirty-five, aging in LA, *per se,* is the most mortifying reality of all, trumping, I think it fair to say, even death. In fact, there are both men and women whose faces are so frozen by Botox they might already be wearing their own death masks; and yet beneath those complexions full of strange repose reside brains full of the most neuralogic complexity.

In any case, as she was chatting in his ear about a restaurant review in the *LA Times,* yet another udon eatery, he was vaguely nodding, his eyes trailing off and inward to what you guessed were the homicidal commerce zones of his brain, where she clearly was not invited and wouldn't care to go even if she were, as whatever he did there was his bloody business, so long as the toasted-just-right pumpkin bread and impeccably steeped jasmine pearl tea, from the gorgeous scent of it, kept coming. I cringed at how not too long ago I was also part of the mindless twittering and fondling and flouting of this new restaurant or that new clothing or gourmet store; the adolescent enthusiasm and endless rallying of each other into a fundamentalist like belief that all the remorseless trendy vacuity was actually food for the soul. This new Oaxacan or all-you-can-eat Korean, or so-called "taco" truck; or that new in–your-face carnivore place, or ceviche bar where they shuck the shells and stone grind the herbs and pour in the lemon and lime and other flavorsome juices to order at your table (it was a recipe/technique, the owner told you, he *borrowed* from a little old Mexican lady on the sandy, and no doubt also seaweed and fecal stinking beach near Barra de Potosi). Hey, how about that wine bar or cupcake or four-dollars-a-stroke donut store?

These venues weren't there to enjoy, but rather there to be pissed on; I pissed there two weeks before you pissed there and my friend is pissing there next week again, though we understand it takes three months to piss there now, whereas when it first opened you could just walk in and piss whenever you wanted. Last month I pissed there three times in one week alone, and in August friends of ours are coming in from New York, which will give us a chance to piss there together, the least we could do since they invited us to piss at their favorite five-star when we were in New York—not to give the impression that we are in a pissing contest or anything. But for all the places one marked with one's piss, one could just as well unmark it in a lick; a few small missteps, and suddenly people were yakking and Yelping it to death, zipping and lining up to piss somewhere else. As she read a paragraph on the earthy richness of this new udon palace's broth, in prose so highfalutin it might've served to celebrate an occasion of national consequence, the husband, or whatever significant other he was, remained turned in to the point of vanishing.

I now recalled how when I first entered the industry, I used to meet hard-charging and boisterous execs who regularly convened for smarmy martini hours, and swapped stories about mistresses, did poker night on occasion, and cut out for golf twice a week, but now they seemed to have all but died or misshapen into measured butchers, cowards, turned utterly in on themselves and their avarice, left only to scheme how to better truncheon X, Y, or Z at the next business luncheon. Anymore—thinking again of Juicy Couture—they've become twig-collecting minions for a vast nest engineered for a species of permanently pregnant yet, ironically, anorexic birds.

I made a quick survey of the middle-aged men I knew and concluded they were mostly zombies, spiritually gutted zombies, shuffling forward to the drumbeat of *more more more*, waiting to see what direction *more* would turn, this way then that; decadent little high-pitched eunuchs that in one instant might opine on a thousand shades of Syrah and serve your head up on a platter the next.

Speaking of platters, I needed to order. The French Onion Soup, or so they quaintly called it, was featured on the appetizer menu. *There was no way a soup that was as pedestrian as French Onion could possibly survive here*, I thought. The chef will undoubtedly render it to the point of ridicule and unrecognizability, just as chefs around the city render to the point of ridicule and unrecognizability any simple homespun dish they touch. You imagined the outlandish ingredients—subtropical onions steeped for a fortnight in authentic Mayan urns, topped with cheese sourced from the nether regions of Nederland, and finished with shaved truffles from some Normandy forest rooted up by swine whose bloodline trace back to Charlemagne's private petting zoo—but still, at fifteen bucks it seemed like my best bet and maybe, too, they'd bring a basket of the scrumptious looking bread. I ordered it.

No, if you were a single or divorced man over the age of forty who didn't own a Lamborghini, you might as well hang it up in a city like this. Married or not, for the vast balance of middle-aged–middle-class men, the ego bludgeoning of daily life in LA is nearly unendurable and, I must add, insurmountable, as the usual places of refuge, dingy bars and pubs and coffee shops, have become all but outlawed here; drop into the city by happenchance and you'd have to comb the streets for hours to simply find a comfortable and reasonably priced bar for a guy to get away from the maw without having to endure the humiliation of a hundred magnificent human peacocks strutting about and yawping. We've virtually emptied the city of sanctuaries where you can pat your big belly, or scratch your hairy chest, or wag your heavy head, where you can enjoy the simple sloppy company of other men just as exhausted by the contraption.

On the hormonal pressure cooker, we've welded even the steam release-valve of football shut. Towns across the country hardly large enough to host a cotillion ball, virtual hamlets, have managed to accommodate football, but to merely suggest we would suffer the game, its soiled, stinking, plebian, pigskin exudation-celebration, amounts to an indignity. The only type of violence suffered here is digital violence, even though real violence is gutting the city in all its mundane mercilessness at every corner and at every hour. The very people that passionately fashion a thousand different apocalypses—writers and producers and directors—those that dream of torture, murder, and mayhem, day and night, get whacked out of shape if you should mentally tax a lab rat.

But truly, our attitude toward football best elucidates this city's hypocrisy. We hated the Rams and Raiders and were relieved when they left; let's face it: we hated football, because football reeks of rutting, and rutting reeks of sex, and sex reeks of corruption, and corruption reeks of dissolution, and dissolution reeks of death. There is not a TV show, reality or otherwise, whose jokes and plots are so thoroughly steeped in sex that just fifty years ago they justified R or even X, and yet for all that sexuality and seduction, LA may be the most frostiest place on the planet to the simplest human humping.

You could more easily get fucked just about anywhere, I thought, looking longingly at the lovely hostess who—three martinis in and screw my car, apparently—I was hell-bent on assigning a starring role to in my newest romantic drama, confected on demand in the dining room of the Chateau! No, in Los Angeles you will find the highest order of human loneliness, indeed, loneliness unrivalled in the annals of human intimacy. In any other place and time the sad diffuse feeling that is loneliness is simply explained, but in Los Angeles the feeling is a phantom paradox that people lie awake charging their brains to bring to form. *How could I be in the middle of a city with thousands of people just like me, just as young, attractive, and friendly as me, just as intelligent and ambitious and sexually stirring as me, and yet be so crushingly alone!*

Just watch the testosterone and estrogen misery jammed into any number of bars on any given Thursday night, all laughing and quaffing and exchanging numbers, all to no avail, as all but a handful are waiting to ravish a handful of apparitions that naturally fail to materialize, I thought, waiting for my French Onion Soup, waiting for Lipchitz. So deft is the art of summing up a potential sexual partner, so sensitively tuned and even preprogrammed is the sexual summing up abacus in the male Hollywood type's brain, barely a sideway glance is enough to size up an entire bar full of women against the information filled fulcrums of light, refracted, jiggered, intensified to mind-bending perfection that have supplanted what in any other city would qualify as prom queen material.

The end result: at last call, from the cords of men dry humping their stupid barstools you could almost spark a bonfire. Not that these otherwise-prom-queens would come, so to speak, if called. For a vast proportion of industry girls, sex is not about releasing from life's mortifying slog into the transcendent pleasures of the flesh, but rather about building up a solid portfolio; *I fucked so-and-so who owns this and that club, or codirected this or that movie, or is besties with a b-lister; and just the other day I licked the cunt of a chick who is going in for her third audition for whatever*; in the manner of an ivy school candidate every sexual "i" and "t" must be dotted and crossed so that one can be corrupted by the administration, even down to the assistant to the assistant dean, when the big casting call finally arrives. In respect to simple carnal enjoyment in this city, the flesh obsessiveness of our first puritan pilgrims comes to mind: let the savages freely copulate, but not we; we, of an otherworldly order, are charged to hone our craft, endure endless hardships and earthly degradation, and—most of all—lay mortal pleasure fallow, so that our semen and saliva and pussy juice might be used to better hallow this angelic land.

I took a serious swig of my martini, kind of
laughing, and thought, even that's not quite right:
they don't loathe sex, but rather the horror of the
afterglow, as this sweet, faint flickering of the flesh
amid the quietly smoldering embers and finest
human soot, adumbrates our mortal exhaustion,
the folly of the ego, its ambition and aims and,
most of all, it is the simple stealing away of energy
needed to power the lantern. From the want of
human touch, so fragile and high-strung are some
of these girls that they've effectively become high
art: brush up against one, even by accident, and
you'll find them emotionally storming toward
you like one of those museum guards at The Met.

Inevitably, though, it gets too much, and as
the crow's-feet show and a few grays appear, these
self-abnegating madonnas morph into sweet and
sexy, and often quite intelligent and energetic,
industry exec sluts. Those stunning, early-thir-
ty-something girls in their hybrid Caddies, dart-
ing into Holy Foods for sulfate-free shampoo;
those eco-conscious soccer moms—married to
or divorced (should enough joint equity accrue)
from one or another exec—were, plain and simple, once-upon-a-time industry sluts and whores.
There are thousands of hot ex-industry exec
MILFs with new boobs and even tightened va-

ginas, fucking the brains out of surfer blond boy toys, whereas when they were married it was all *I'm tired* and *Once my period is over* or *I just need a little romance*, as in The Caribbean or Jackson Hole. At any number of Hollywood parties you can find the ego-shrapneled standing in the corner and wondering how to carry on with his dull hemorrhaging self without the hot blonde standing statuesquely there next to him for ballast. So obvious what she was in it for, because what the fuck would a hot blonde with a bikini begging body do with a balding, and actually quite boring guy thirty pounds over weight and twenty years her senior, if not to filet his financial portfolio at its fleshiest.

I came up from these thoughts, to see the handsome middle-aged Jonathan Clubish man mumbling something beneath his breath and studying his fingers that he was clenching and stretching rheumatically, as in, "What will come of my asphyxiation skills?" Juicy tapped his arm to get his attention and a smile automatically reshaped on his jaded face, like she'd just pressed a *smile* button.

Now, I imagined him—and sheer imagination it was—hardly a dynamic, avaricious Hollywood exec calculating his next ruthless business move, but rather a has-been exec, quietly pining, just like me not too long ago, over his human superfluity, what he had lost, and with every passing day what he was less and less likely to recover. There were countless execs like him with once powerful gravities that were knocked off course by some random cosmic perturbation and left to drift like orphaned planets through the most pitiless outer space. Stars, too, dozens whom you personally knew, reduced to white dwarves with maybe one or two desiccated orbs, near human mothballs, still hanging pathetically on at the edges. From repeated dissing, you imagined, he is now disintegrating right there at the Chateau; disintegrating in the midst of, if not precisely because of, its monotonous and trance inducing beauty.

I recalled how from the purest sense of desperation and exile I retreated further and further into my iPhone address book, like a naked mole foraging for corms. I called one person and then another, all of my hundreds of elaborate connections and networks, greased for years with glad handing and near happy endings, dwindling to a few far flung orderlies amazed that a person of my caliber and former station would be calling on them for aid. An assistant director on a daytime soap (whose meager clout I had strangely fetishized) was the final straw, as if with each call, nine in all, I was lining up for him another mirror hit, until it became agonizingly obvious that my desperation was his most perverse addiction; eventually, even he was repulsed and the whole exchange deteriorated into *look, why don't I call you when I hear something.* Should I have queried Siri on the matter? I'm sure even she, my most patient retainer, would've voiced revulsion.

Then there were the calls I continued to get from people asking me for leads, people whom I hadn't seen in years, precisely and perversely as the people I'd been calling hadn't seen me in years, the sum of it like the famished asking for a handout from the starving. Yet did I simply say, *I can't help you?* No, I did not: I hemmed and hawed and rappelled to the nether abysses of my brain, because perhaps there was someone after all I hadn't dredged up that might be of service to this poor bastard and this poor bastard's project. What an embarrassment. They kept calling me, just as I'd kept calling others, until I too was forced more or less to say, *Look, why don't I call you when I hear something.* And here was my French Onion Soup.

The waiter placed it in front of me and said, "Enjoy," and could he get me anything else.

"Thank you. I think this will do for now; it looks delicious," which it did, though perhaps the sheer oniony smell of it just then mirrored too perfectly the onionyness of my thoughts, so much so that I pushed it aside and stayed with my martini.

This city is ready for a script like yours, though, in truth, you've moved beyond this script—or, rather, one part of you has moved beyond it and the other part of you is still, evidently, waffling. I opened *Left in the Dark*, which, as every line was virtually trademarked in my brain, I hadn't bothered to read in months. I read one page, then two, and then to page fifteen and stopped, in a near panic. Awful! I read three pages more: all of it drenched in the most syrupy seriousness and spite.

What made you think you could get away with writing a movie like this anyway? Sure, though Hollywood enjoys some occasional sadomasochistic cudgeling, as in *The Player* or *LA Confidential*, the vast majority of movies that rip it a new one hardly stand a chance. But would Lipchitz want to meet up merely to tell you that your script is lousy? Hollywood producers barely meet with writers to tell them their script is brilliant. Lipchitz isn't inclined to meet at all unless he's already thought through from top to below bottom what he has in his ruthless mind. There is probably nothing in the least wrong with your script. Only its aura has waned, just as auras are prone to do when they sit in gloomy seclusion for months on end. Any script's aura both waxes and wanes, in fact, it's a kind of living thing whose aura is brightened or dimmed by the temperament or intelligence or especially SOBERNESS of the reader, even if that reader is the writer. Put a work of genius in the hands of a dimwit and the dimwit will think that work of genius dimwitted. How many times have you fallen out of love with a script you were madly in love with just months earlier? That's because where you are now is not where you were when you wrote the script; but where you were then might very well be where everybody else is now, the reason, obviously, that Lipchitz wanted to meet.

I breathed a little easier and looked for the beautiful receptionist. There she was, so polished and so perceptive. No, the majority of Angelenos feel precisely as you feel, and this script reflects that feeling precisely, but a part of you no longer feels this way, indeed, the very best part of you, the part of you that moved to that space, even hearth, let's say, that Hirschman had built and left behind,

I thought, sitting there at the Chateau still slavishly waiting for Lipchitz.

Maybe this script is about *your* fear and rejection and disappointments and has nothing at all to do with Hollywood. There's never been a novelist that has been able to write about LA, and anyone who ever starts to write about it ultimately ends up writing about himself—(Hirschman). This is why I had to get out of the city; because I finally realized that each of the five books I'd written about Los Angeles had actually been books I'd written about myself, virtual memoirs—(Hirschman). Imagine, just imagine finding a metaphor for God, and you will know what I mean; how ridiculous the metaphor would prove, because the moment you find a metaphor for God you are by definition finding a metaphor for yourself—(Hirschman).

I downed the balance of my martini to get out from under Hirschman's remarks; a stupid thing to do, because even before it hit my stomach, impossibly, it seemed, I was a degree tipsier, when I needed to be more clear headed than ever. I now recalled at one point early in my career, Hirschman advising me to read and reread my scripts before submitting them to my agent: read it and revise it, happy and sad, apathetic, drunk and hung-over, because each state of being is actually a new window onto the work.

Then, like a new window had opened onto the very reason for this meeting, I thought, maybe Lipchitz wanted to talk about another project he had in the works, a rewrite, or to take me on for a book he'd optioned.

NO, *this is all wrong*, the suddenly and unexpectedly intelligent lush in me snapped. Since Lipchitz texted a week ago, he's had second thoughts about your script and was inch by ugly inch, as is the habit with industry execs, cancelling. Maybe he thought well of the script, maybe he was taken in by it for a spell, but then sent it to an associate who told him, "Is this really a good time to be burning bridges, Saul?"

Anyway, idiot, you should know by now that when someone in LA says, "Let's meet up," they actually mean, "Unless one of my dozen other simultaneous, but more important, appointments comes through." You should know by now that in LA when they say, "I love it," they actually mean, "It's 'okay,' as okay as a dozen other scripts sitting on my desk." In LA, when someone says, "Definitely," they mean "Most likely not." In LA, when someone says, "Let's think about it," they mean, "Thank god I've got that one off my plate."

In LA, when someone says, "Let's get together," they mean, "See you when I next see you by sheer chance." In LA, when someone says, "This is a serious script," they are saying, "Maybe you should try another racket!"

There is an entire lobotomizing, neurotic, nearly Masonic code of communication in LA, whereby nothing anyone says means what he or she said, but rather often means the opposite. If someone says, "Yes," no matter how enthusiastically, indeed, particularly if enthusiastically, you must have a dozen contingencies plans for, "No;" a schizophrenic mode of communication that you find up and down the ladder of success, but that often reaches its apex smack in the middle among the—kind-of-successful-but-not-really—all-that types that are still near enough to the lower rungs to feel, and naturally exploit for erotic pleasure, the kinetic tongues of a thousand aspirants lapping at them from below.

On the last day of my visit, Hirschman drove me out to Red Top, a good twenty-minute drive down Avenue 18 ½ on the north side of Madera heading west, a long-seemingly interminable stretch of road dead in the middle of the country where vast flat alfalfa fields opened up with bales interspersed like huge uniform gravestones.

Hirschman said, "I've saved very little money since I've moved here; hundreds of dollars in gas in a single month exploring the back roads of the Great Central Valley, documenting, just because they are so beautiful, hundreds of farmhouses and small water towers and barns; great piles of branches ready to burn after pruning, and, because of this drought, fields of trees torn from their roots and laid to rest like fallen soldiers."

He'd taken hundreds of photos during these outings: a mist hanging over a cotton field, the sun setting the tops of almond trees ablaze, the explosion of colors in Spring, pink, red, and especially white that topped the branches like thick fallen snow. As though he were touring his own future for the both of us, we passed probably a dozen small shrines set up on the shoulder of the road that marked, Hirschman told me, where fatal accidents had occurred. A good many were pitched at crossroads—in front of telephone poles and big cylindrical cement structures, where well water burbled up—and all had crosses, some wreathed with plastic flowers, and others with a framed picture of the Virgin, or the departed, with tall jar candles set at the base. Most were dulled from standing out there for who knows how long, and others were fresh as if planted there the day before.

"Forget about stoplights, the country roads barely have stop signs, plenty barely standing, and even though for the most part they're spaced half a mile apart, that's a rule of thumb, it's just as likely they will pop up out of nowhere," he said. Hirschman pointed down the road and said, "Owl," then we passed it perched on a fence post, and as though they were longtime neighbors, "Morning," he said.

"Dirt lanes cutting across the farms intersect these roads every few hundred yards, and if a tractor driver isn't careful, all he has to do is punch the pedal a little too hard and he's nosed onto that road, with God only knows what barreling his way. In winter, fog gets so thick, if you pause for a piss you might very well lose sight of your dick. Even how far you've travelled is weirdly lost in that fog, like you aren't so much moving ahead as churning in porridge."

They appeared out of nowhere, these makeshift shrines, but, what also felt to me, at regular intervals, almost as though one to the other they were there to tell a story, like the Stations of the Cross.

I looked up from these reminisces of Hirschman and saw the time was approaching 2:15. Lipchitz obviously wasn't going to show. I knew it an hour ago, I realized, but was only now conceding it, only partly due to the buzz. The pretty receptionist would surmise precisely what had happened. She'd seen the same scene unfold a hundred times, and had likely experienced it first hand. No doubt he'll text in an hour or so and concoct some or other excuse and add, *let's reschedule—let me look at my calendar when I'm back in my office and I'll let you know.* With that, he will put you away; perhaps for the time being, perhaps forever—it was his call and your job was to take it whenever and however into you're A-hole it came.

I signaled for the waiter and asked for my check.

"The bottom line about those roads," Hirschman said, "is you more or less have to feel your way through by a kind of instinct, but even then, at certain times of the year in hail or crazy rain, or, like I told you already, fog thick as feta, it's just a tad better than playing Russian roulette. That, alongside the reality that farm workers, accounting for ninety-nine percent of these disasters, typically drive cars that barely deserve the name, more like contrivances that by hook or crook torque forward, and when a wheel drops from one of those pushing seventy on a country road with no shoulder to speak of, you're not sittin' very pretty. Plus, let's lay it all on the table, there's nothing better than a six-pack of Coronas after eight hours of picking plums. To top it off, imagine double axles, ten tons of steel and fruit, flying down these roads by drivers in a rush to beat the heat; even the law requires they lay off the wheel after twelve hours, plenty pop a Benny or just keeping hauling ass one eye shut: halfway through harvest half the time they're at the wheel half asleep. In fact, amazing how few people die out here; honestly, can't help but feel grace—sheer grace keeps most people through a season safe."

Way in front of us now was the coast Range Mountains, a rolling grayish blue, like a snapshot of a wave. Hirschman just then confessed that though all he'd done over the course of his career is write about LA, in the end he'd never written a single word about LA. Only out here, he said, only from this distance was I able to see that there was no way to write effectively from inside the city, because not only did one rarely have the luxury of quieting down enough to write effectively from inside the city, but also and mostly, because one was always cognizant of being watched in the city *even if, and especially if, one was never being watched,*" (a construction that took me some time to unpack).

"The whole of society has now become absolutely comfortable with being watched, in fact, they expect and even yearn to be watched, thus we have what can only be described as a soft surveillance state, or rather a stateless surveillance state, looking over and even into us *even when it isn't, indeed, especially when it isn't.* This willingness, even yearning to be invaded this way is one of the most radical about-faces of the modern age, pitching us back into little village life, and all the self-monitoring, obsessive self-control, and therefore retarding of all our inner reality and all its generative power. It's always been the case that the isolation and even loneliness, the inward motion required to produce any great work of art is utterly absent in the city because of the noisy sucking rattle, but in the last few years it has gotten even worse. At least for the last ten years I was always someone watch myself living in the city, and the reason for that is because I was watching them watching me, especially when they weren't watching me," Hirschman said.

"Sure, there were times, at night, early in the wee hours, when the streets were empty, that I felt all this watching wane, and the sweetest privacy and quietude grow, even if the kind one finds in the middle of the perennial hurricane. It was at these moments I loved the city for all the reasons that it deserved to be loved: the steady patience of its climate, the natural unfolding of its hills, and the luxurious quality of its light; but year to year these moments became fewer and fewer until they seemed to have disappeared entirely. But what is happening in LA is happening, because of LA, one is even tempted to say, everywhere. In lieu of a beating heart, cities across the globe are establishing into their particular stratospheres an enormous everlasting eye, a kind of satellite-eye whereby every single eye below shoots up a signal that is reflected down and transmitted to every other eye, a virtual *omniopticon*. The million windows looking outward toward the unknown have turned into a million eyes looking inward to the point of paralysis or farce. It is like each of us are standing in a hall of mirrors, where into infinity we find ourselves and disappear at the same time. Like I said before, maybe in a year or two I will waken only to discover that I have escaped to the same place even here in the middle of nowhere," Hirschman said, "because, let's face it, the machine in all its crushing reality is now no longer a machine, no longer a lumbering rattling numbing contraption, one we can point to, rise up on and toss or crush, but rather a specter that affects your way of thinking, your inner disposition so deeply and so artfully we can no longer even hear its hum."

"Look," he said, and pointed to four hawks circling in the distance. We watched them one by one dive to snatch their prey. "Likely," he said, "field mice, but maybe gophers. Anyway, I will stay here," he said, "until I can extract myself and fashion a hearth. Whether it's possible or not is, of course, an open question, and one each of us, I'm afraid, must answer, should we even dare to ask it: because what we are involved with here is the contemporary version of what we can only fairly describe as a spiritual problem."

We crossed a bridge spanning a dried up riverbed, and soon all that lushness began to disappear, and soon it was as desolate as a desert, great expanses of empty dirt where here and there small twisters moved. "Behold the drought," Hirschman said. We'd come to a place that just a season or two ago was, Hirschman told me, "Bountiful as Eden."

I paid the bill in cash and stood and glanced at the beautiful waitress one last time. To my surprise, she was just then looking at me, and so I nodded and a little smile lifted on her beautiful face, and then I headed out, pausing, I must sickeningly confess, in front of the elevator and its old-fashioned dial, where a haunting presence, the diabolical doppelgänger, perhaps, of the very presence Hirschman felt in Forestiere's cave, beckoned me to re-consider: maybe I should have one more drink, maybe the battery on his old Black-Berry had died, or he'd got stuck in one of those cellular limbo zones; maybe I will see him coming in as I'm going out, I thought, before I snatched myself away from the degradation and turned for the street. The air was calm and crisp and youthful, as usual; across the street, only yards away from the thunder and exhaust of Sunset Boulevard, the latest novitiates were lunching on the sidewalk, under umbrellas, smiling and drinking, toasting and boasting, oblivious and blissful as could be. I'd taken Sunset three times by bike to the beach when I was in my late teens, peddling through Beverly Hills, Westwood, handsome Brentwood, and finally making my way to the winding and windy Palisades where, between the cliffs, the ocean opened up in front of me, a kind of aquatic altar that marked the end of the continent, but also marked the end of time as we humans knew it. No matter how many boats or bodies we threw at it, it would forever remain, eternally recurring, changing, and yet always the same, there as it always had been and always would be, even when I wasn't. I hopped in my ja-lopy and joined the west-heading throng. There was not a beep; *introibo ad altare Dei*, one and all, wending snakewise to eternity, it seemed, patient as penitents waiting their turn for the wine and the wafer.